AVALON
~ WEB OF MAGIC ~
BOOK 6

Trial by Fire

by Rachel Roberts

red sky
PUBLISHING

CDS Books

Text copyright © 2002 by Red Sky Entertainment, Inc.
All rights reserved. Published by CDS Books.

ISBN 1-59315-008-3

10 9 8 7 6 5 4 3 2 1

First CDS Books printing, June 2003

Printed in the U.S.A.

Chapter 1

Dark clouds slid over twin moons, covering the night like a blanket. Behind the swirling veil, stars fell like tears as earth, mountain, and sky faded away.

A lone howl pierced the blackness.

Sweet smells of fresh grass, cool springs, and new life filled the air. Above, colors rippled across the heavens as if strewn by some painter's wild brush. Fiery reds, ocean blues, brilliant yellow-greens, purplish red-oranges, deep forest greens curled and danced, a pulsating patchwork that flowed across the sky.

Faint howls, a chorus of spirits echoed from the past, rising into one song, the collective song of ages, the wolfsong.

Run with us!

The ground trembled as hooves pounded the earth. Mistwolves, hundreds, then thousands strong, thundered across the sky.

Swept into the song of the mistwolves, the

power of the mystical vision grew. Towering canyons, fertile plains, immense forests rich and full of life swept past as the pack came upon the land's edge, where sand and sea met, where worlds joined. Thousands of mistwolves stood upon the beachhead. Before them great crystalline towers rose, catching glints of sun and spray. Giant interlocking rocks set in an immense jigsaw puzzle led the way to the crystal city at the edge of forever. Creatures of untold power and magic inhabited the city, sharing its wonders with the world of humans. Families of griffins and dragons circled the skies. Unicorns big and small ran free through the resplendent gardens playing with human students of magic. Sea dragons and merfolk crested the waves, gesturing and smiling as the pack stood.

My spirit sings to be with you! the lone mistwolf cried out.

Take from the past and lead us into the future, Moonshadow.

Lightning flashed, splitting the past from future. The images faded like tracks in the dust.

Moonshadow, leader of the mistwolves, sat alone on the peak of Mount Hope. Tilting his head toward Aldenmor's twin moons, the mighty pack leader tried to draw as much strength from his ancestors as he could. But the vision had ended. Once tens of thousands strong, the pack now numbered only a hundred. Since the erosion of magic from Aldenmor, the wolves had been hunted, feared as enemies, and slaughtered by creatures that had risen in the shadows of darkness. With his ears pressed back, Moonshadow felt what his ancestors had once felt. He knew what they had known. The mistwolves were strong, proud protectors. Then, as now, they were the guardians of Aldenmor.

At last, the mistwolf opened his golden eyes. Moonshadow's heart ached. The once glorious realm of Aldenmor lay before him in ruins — ravaged by black fire, devoid of trees and grass, burned and scarred from the dark magic.

Moonshadow howled into the wind, crying for what was lost. For a moment, his cry lingered, echoing across the Shadowlands. Then, all was silent.

Moonshadow knew then what his spirit vision meant. The pack's images spoke of hope, of humans and magical creatures working together as in ancient times. Moonshadow held the sliver of renewed hope to his chest as he shook the morning dew from his coat. He felt the cool object dangling around his neck. The fairy map, a magical talisman given to him by the fairimentals and Adriane, his human wolf sister. He'd been using the fairy map to guide the pack through the portals on Aldenmor in an attempt to defend the land from the Dark Sorceress. She was rapidly destroying the planet, draining magic, and storing it in giant crystals deep underground in the dark circle of the Shadowlands. The crystal constructions were dangerous and difficult to complete — each successive attempt to twist the magic had caused massive black fire fallout — but as Moonshadow had seen in his vision, not impossible. Even with the help of the map, the battle to protect Aldenmor was being slowly lost. Time and magic were running out.

The facets of the talisman flashed and twinkled in the rays of the morning sun. Moonshadow thought again of his vision and suddenly wondered if the map had been given to him for a different purpose altogether.

If only he could contact the fairimentals. They would know what he was supposed to do, but the Fairy Glen had been cut off. No one had been able to reach it or the fairimentals for weeks.

Suddenly, the fur on the back of Moonshadow's neck stood up. He sniffed at the air. Something smelled foul. Perhaps wafts of further decay from the Shadowlands — the howl cut through his thoughts as a gray mistwolf broke through the brush.

"Come quickly," the wolf called, *"the mistwolves are under attack."* Moonshadow leaped to his feet

and turned toward his approaching wolf brother. *"Who dares to attack the mistwolves?"* the leader asked.

"I do," the mistwolf replied, fiercely baring long, sharp teeth.

Moonshadow tensed. But before he could move, searing pain lanced across his shoulder. He fell to his knees as pain washed over him in waves of agony. Snarling and short of breath, he saw the riders appear, as if out of thin air. Thick bodies sat heavily on their mounts, eyes gleaming menacing green through the ports of steel helmets. Sharp serrated teeth grinned wildly from stout heads with pointed ears. They wore leather armor and spiked boots and held long whips that dripped venomous green poison. Goblins. And they were riding nightmares. The fiendish giant mounts snorted bursts of fire as their eyes glowed demon red. Jet black imps dangled glowing nets between them.

Ropes could not hold a mistwolf — even this traitor should know that. Moonshadow concentrated on releasing his physical body free of its corporal trappings. He closed his eyes and summoned his magic, waiting for the feeling of lightness that came when he turned to mist. But he couldn't. He felt locked in place, as if something was controlling his magic.

The enchanted net flew over the giant wolf. He

felt fire digging into his sides, tightening around his neck. He desperately tried to turn to mist, but every struggle increased the nets' hold over him.

His haunches were caught and pulled tight, slamming the wolf to the ground.

"White Fang! Dream Runner!" Moonshadow howled in fury.

"Don't bother," the gray wolf snarled, as he watched the struggling pack leader. *"We've already taken care of the others. You're the last."*

The riders shouted in oblique, rough tongues as their nightmares snorted, encircling the wolf. The pack leader made no further move to escape, knowing that his struggles would only suffocate him. Instead, he slowed his panting and moved his mind away from the pain. Growling low, he tried to see past the nightmares' long legs. He needed to identify the traitor.

Moonshadow locked eyes with the wolf that had dared to betray the pack. The net was yanked tight as the goblin riders pulled the wolf leader down hard. But Moonshadow no longer felt the pain. He kept his eyes on the traitor wolf.

The goblin riders jeered before kicking their mounts, dragging Moonshadow quickly behind them.

Alone on the peak, the traitor watched the riders disappear into the valley of dark shadows below. Golden eyes flickered fiery red as smooth fur shimmered, dissolving into scales. The wolf's body flowed and twisted as it rose up on its two hind legs. A lizard-shaped head twisted free with a mouthful of pointed teeth. Long scaly legs with splayed feet stood tall, and webbed claws sharpened into nails as the Skultum resumed his true form.

Chapter 2

Kara Davies watched the fire dance behind the ornate wrought-iron screen. The fireplace tools stood to the right in a metal basket tipped with animal claws. The sides of the hearth were trimmed with stone wings. Just about everything in Ravenswood Manor had been inspired or influenced by animals. Some were easily recognizable like the famous wildlife paintings of lions hunting the Serengeti Plain, Siberian tigers from India, massive grizzlies from the Canadian northwest, wild horses running across the open Dakota plains. Other objects hinted at more unusual creatures — a unicorn engraving in the wood paneling, a dragonhead of ebony set on chair arms. If you didn't know better, these were merely decorative touches inspired by fanciful myths and legends.

But Kara Davies, Emily Fletcher, and Adriane Charday knew that fantastic creatures like these still existed in a magical world called Aldenmor. At one time, these amazing creatures were plentiful. But

8

like so many great species of Earth caught forever frozen in paintings and pieces of ornamental art, there were very few, if any, real ones left.

Perhaps that was why the guardians of the magical world, known as fairimentals, had sent for the girls, enfolding them in a mystery as profound as the magic itself. Three among millions had been chosen, gifted with the magic. Their lives were now bound forever with animals and creatures they used to think only lived in fairy tales.

Shadows coiled across the rows of stacked books as Kara took in warmth and comfort from the Ravenswood Manor library. She gazed out the large windows that looked upon the great lawn behind the manor house. Many creatures had come to Ravenswood for refuge. The animals out there weren't paintings, they were real. So many. Endangered and lost. How could she, Emily, and Adriane protect them when they were just learning about the magic themselves? How could she help them when she couldn't even help herself?

Lyra, the big orange spotted cat, arched her back and stretched her long front legs. *"You're thinking again,"* she purred.

"I do have a brain, you know," the blond-haired girl quipped. "Contrary to popular opinion."

"I didn't say anything."

Kara regarded the computer station on one of

the shelves of the library wall. When the girls were not using the library as their clubhouse, the computer remained hidden behind a sliding bookcase.

Ozzie had been one of the first magical animals to arrive here. In Aldenmor, he'd been an elf. Now, he was stuck in a ferret's body. A very smart ferret! Now Ozzie quickly turned back to the data he was reviewing. The list of animals scrolling down the screen had grown since the girls had first met the magical ferret back at the end of August. Some fifty creatures, big and small, now resided here along with deer, peacocks, monkeys, and birds. There were a lot of animals to watch over. Winter was coming. Normally at this time of year, Kara was all about Thanksgiving with friends and family, Christmas trees, parties and presents, ice-skating, and hot chocolate. Now all she thought about was how they were going to feed so many hungry and cold creatures. Depressing thoughts. This was her responsibility. She had convinced her father, the mayor of Stonehill, to let the girls take care of Ravenswood. So many were counting on her, and so far, she had failed miserably.

Lyra sat up and looked at Kara. *So many sad thoughts.*

"Oh." Kara's expression softened. Though the room was toasty warm, Kara shivered at the memory of what had happened at the Ravenswood Benefit Concert last weekend. She had dabbled in a form of magic called spellsinging, and it had backfired big-time. She had fallen under the spell of an evil shape-shifter who had used her to open the Ravenswood portal — the magical door that connected Earth to the magic web and to Aldenmor.

Her friends had saved her. By spellsinging together, Emily and Adriane had broken the spell and helped Kara banish the shape-shifter and close the Ravenswood portal after it. But there were other portals, and Kara had no idea what had happened to them. Were they open still? And where did they lead? She couldn't help but feel the path was manipulated by the Dark Sorceress herself, the evil witch who'd caused the destruction of Aldenmor and the poisoning of its inhabitants. A path that could only lead to one place: Avalon, the home of all magic.

Since then, Kara had fallen into despair, questioning her ability to do anything right and her role as a blazing star. And underneath it all was the fear that she was changing, careening away from her life as it had been before magic, plunging headlong into some other weird place.

"I just finished unloading three truckloads of supplies!" Adriane's voice cut through Kara's thoughts as the dark-haired girl bounded into the library followed by Stormbringer, the mistwolf. "Where were you?"

"I was doing some homework." Kara casually gestured to her pile of closed schoolbooks neatly stacked on the oak reading table.

Adriane opened her mouth to comment, but Storm stopped her with a gentle nudge. Adriane shrugged and flopped onto one of the large velvet pillows on the sofa, pulling Storm into a big hug. The great silver mistwolf sprawled over the girl.

"That was a good run." Though the wolf didn't speak out loud, Adriane heard Storm clearly in her head. Lyra could communicate in the same way.

"Gran's had us running all over the place," Adriane said. "Salt strips had to be set up for the deer, and I had to prepare food blends to include turkey, pheasants, quail . . . and quiffles."

Kara wasn't listening. She just stared into the crackling fire.

Adriane frowned. She had never seen Kara like this before. And she didn't like it. They had come a long way together in a few months. When she'd first met Kara, she thought her shallow as a rain puddle. Now she knew that underneath that perfectly coordinated exterior was a real brain, a real heart, and some incredible magical power. Kara was truly a blazing star.

Emily was a natural healer. In the beginning, she helped Kara and Adriane see eye-to-eye, which hadn't been easy. Adriane's warrior temper wasn't easy to keep in check. But in the end, what mattered was that they had taken care of one another and against all odds, forged an unspoken bond of friendship.

Everyone was concerned about Kara's unusual depression, aware of how deeply the spell had affected her. Even her friends at school had noticed Kara's obvious retreat from the normal boisterous, self-assured, perfect being of total cool.

Suddenly, the door burst open. "Mail call!" Emily Fletcher announced as she hurried inside. "Get yer latest copy of the *Stonehill Gazette*."

A small herd of creatures followed the bundled redheaded girl, including Ronif, Balthazar, and Rasha, trusted magical friends. While the pegasi, quiffles, and wommels warmed themselves in front of the fire, Emily dropped her backpack to rub her hands together. Her cheeks were pink with cold. "How's it going, Ozzie?" She looked over the ferret's head as he pounded away on the keys.

"I put all the new E-mails in your "to be answered" file. Ozzie, the fuzzy former elf, had become quite a pro on the computer. He loved dealing with all the E-mail from the fans of Ravenswood. Ozzie had also found a very useful place for himself reviewing and cataloging the mass of information Mr. Gardener, the owner of Ravenswood, had left behind before vanishing.

"Take a break. Look what I brought." Emily pulled four boxes of graham crackers, a dozen chocolate bars, and a bag of marshmallows out of her backpack, dangling the goodies in front of Ozzie's face.

The ferret's eyes practically bugged out of his furry head. "Oooo! What's that?"

"Come on, I'll show you," Emily giggled, walking over to the fireplace.

Ozzie followed her, *and* the tantalizing bag of white marshmallows.

Kara was still staring out the window.

Emily glanced from Kara to Adriane as she pulled out a bunch of long wooden sticks from her pack, handing them to each of the animals.

"The feed supplies arrived," Adriane said, taking a stick and nestling herself between Rommel and Rasha. She deftly stuck a marshmallow onto the end of the stick as the others watched, fascinated.

Ozzie stuffed two marshmallows into his mouth. "YUM!"

"Wait, Ozzie," Emily instructed. "You have to toast the marshmallow and make a sandwich on the crackers."

Adriane, Emily, Ozzie, and the others gathered around the fireplace armed with wooden sticks. "With the new landmark status, the town council has allocated funds for food, but a lot of our animals are just not eating," Adriane said to Ronif.

"They are restless and homesick," Storm said.

"And not everyone is used to cold weather," Ronif the quiffle added. "Most come from warmer climates."

"Ahh!" Ozzie pulled a flaming stick out of the fire, waving it around his head.

"Careful, Ozzie!" Adriane exclaimed, covering her hair.

Ronif and Rasha weren't faring much better, each losing their marshmallows to the hungry flames.

"You're doing it wrong," Kara said softly.

"What?"

"Here. Give me that." Kara took the wooden stick from Ozzie's paw and speared a marshmallow. "You have to lightly brown the marshmallow without letting it burn. See?"

Kara held it over the flame, twirling it lightly until it was golden brown.

"Ooo. That's very good."

"Then," Kara continued. "you place it between *two* layers of chocolate. This way the chocolate covers both graham crackers."

"She's a genius!" Ronif exclaimed.

Emily and Adriane suppressed smiles.

The others, except for Storm and Lyra, followed suit. Soon Ozzie was happily covered in melted marshmallow fluff, chocolate, and crumbs.

Adriane picked up the paper Emily had brought in. The front page displayed a picture of Mrs. Beasley Windor and the town council. Windor was holding a landmark status certificate for Ravenswood. The headline read, RAVENSWOOD A ROARING SUCCESS, PUTS STONEHILL ON THE MAP.

Adriane snorted, "Look at this. Windor hated the idea of Ravenswood from the start, and now she is totally taking credit for our success!"

"That's politics," Emily said. "All things considered, we should be grateful. Why do you think we were able to get the funds for the winter supplies so fast? Windor personally approved the invoices!"

"Yeah, but I still don't have to like it." Adriane threw the paper down.

"Even with the supplies, what if we get more refugees from Aldenmor?" Balthazar, the older pegasi, asked. "We can't turn them away."

Ronif waddled over, testing a marshmallow sandwich in his rubbery beak. "Even with the tours closed for the cold season, someone is bound to discover us."

Emily knew that Ronif was right. Even on a

preserve as big as Ravenswood, they could not hide all of the refugees forever. Although it seemed Mrs. Windor was on their side now, they all knew how quickly things could change.

Kara picked up the newspaper and regarded the picture. Yes, the girls had pulled off the concert and fooled the whole crowd into thinking that the magical battle they saw was all part of the show. But the evil shape-shifting monster pretending to be pop star Johnny Conrad had put Kara under its spell. That was no illusion.

"Kawaaa," Ozzie jumped onto the table, his mouth exploding with marshmallows. "Makemeemee sommmorre!"

"The fairimentals should have made you a pig instead of a ferret," Kara commented.

POP. The fire surged upward in the hearth with a huge crackle, startling the group.

"I've been thinking about the E-mails," Adriane finally said. "I mean, after all this time, why would Gardener and Be*Tween suddenly contact us, and through the computer no less?"

"Maybe they couldn't before," Rasha offered.

"Yes, maybe they were trapped somewhere," Ronif added.

"That's what I was thinking," Adriane said. "Suppose when Kara opened the portals, she freed them. Or at least allowed them to contact us briefly."

17

That caught Kara's interest. "You're saying it's a good thing that I opened the portals?"

"Well, you do have a knack for using magic in unusually lucky ways." Adriane smiled warmly.

"That's a big suppose," Kara snorted, but nonetheless, a sparkle appeared in her eyes. "I still believed in Johnny and got burned big-time."

"But that wasn't your fault," Emily said. "Any one of us would have fallen victim to such strong magic."

"Still, Gardener and Be*Tween didn't give us much information," Ozzie continued, munching another s'more.

"Maybe they couldn't," Rasha said excitedly. "Afraid they might get caught."

"Remember when the fairimentals first came to us at the glade?" Adriane stood and asked.

"Yes," Emily remembered all too well. "They told us to find Avalon."

"And that's what Kara was doing," Adriane continued as she paced in front of the fire.

"Maybe that's what she did!" Ozzie finished.

Kara's eyes flew open wide. "So maybe . . . I did good."

"Kara," Adriane stopped in front of the blond girl. "Whatever you did, we know you *meant* to do good and that's what counts."

"That's right!" Ozzie leaned over the table to

hug the blond girl. "We're always with you no matter what!"

Kara flushed but smiled, holding the gooey ferret away from her sweater. "Thanks." She placed Ozzie back on the rug to toast some more marshmallows.

"The Dark Sorceress means to take the magic from wherever she can get it. It's just a matter of time before Aldenmor is completely destroyed!" Adriane pounded her fist. A quick glance at her friends told Adriane that they were all thinking the same thing. The three had been chosen by the fairimentals to save Aldenmor. Each had magical power and each had a job to do — find Avalon.

"Hey. Watch the fur," Storm rumbled, licking a dollop of melted marshmallow off her shimmering coat.

"Sorry," Ozzie said, holding the stick of marshmallows behind him as he faced the group.

Sparks of fire leaped from the crackling logs, licking at the melting six marshmallows Ozzie had crammed onto a stick.

"Be careful, Ozzie," Ronif complained. "That's hot!"

"And it smells awful." The ferret scrunched his marshmallow mustache, sniffing the air around him. "Smells like —"

"Ozzie!" Emily yelled.

"Your tail's on fire!" Balthazar observed.

"Huh?" Ozzie looked over his shoulder. "Ahhhh!"

The ferret tossed his marshmallows as he ran across the room, a plume of smoke trailing him. Everyone jumped out of the way, grabbing rugs, towels, and anything they could find to throw over the smoking ferret.

"ARG! Gah!"

Kara grabbed a vase from an end table, threw away the flowers, and emptied the water over Ozzie.

"Glub!"

Smoke hissed from the soaked ferret.

"Are you okay, Ozzie?" Emily asked, grabbing and hoisting him upside down to examine his tail.

"Watch it! Watch it!"

"Hold still." Emily's rainbow jewel pulsed with blue healing light. It bathed the ferret in a cool glow. "How's that?"

"Put me down!"

The soft lights in the library flickered and went dark.

The girls looked around. Smoke was slowly encircling the room.

"We blow a fuse?" Adriane asked.

The fireplace blazed, flames leaping high, sending sparks into the air as shadows skittered and crawled across the walls.

Suddenly, the fire hissed and with a loud *POP!,* flames leaped out, licking at the mantel.

The s'more eaters scrambled back.

"The fire's too big!" Adriane yelled.

With a shudder, the flames erupted out of the stone hearth, pushing aside the screen to roll across the rug in a fiery wave.

Hssssssssssss.

Like snakes, tendrils of flame reached up and coiled around itself.

"Get the extinguisher!" Emily yelled.

"Wait," Lyra told the three girls all at once. The big cat was on her feet, fur standing along the scruff of her neck.

"It's not burning anything," Ronif observed.

The fire was now completely outside the fireplace, on the carpet in the center of the room. Strangely, nothing burned. The flames left no mark on what they touched as if the fire were merely a ghost.

Swirling yellow, red, and blue flames reached to the domed ceiling of the library. They formed a figure, shimmering and glowing before the group.

A fairimental!

"Thank goodness, we thought you were lost," Ozzie said to the fire figure, holding on to Emily's neck.

The fire wavered. *"Fairy glennn iss dyinng,"* the flaming figure hissed.

"It's a *firemental!"* Balthazar said, astonished. Everyone looked to the Pegasus. "The most powerful and dangerous of the fairimentals."

"Usssssse mappp," the firemental hissed, reaching out with flaming arms.

A tendril snapped like a whip, flicking at Kara. The blond girl squealed and stepped back. But the flames found her, wrapping around and encasing her in a web of fire. The fire separated into strands, then wove into a ball of flame.

"Stand still, Kara!"

Kara stood motionless as the fire swirled around her.

"It's telling Kara to use the fairy map!" Ozzie yelled.

Kara felt desperate waves of magic flowing, forcing the fire figure to hold together. She barely heard the small voice hissing in her ear.

"Uu mussst findd Avvalonnn," the fire hissed, spattered and flickered out.

"Wait!" Adriane gasped. "Come back."

"Is everyone all right?" Emily scanned the room making sure no one was burned.

"I've never seen anything like that before," Balthazar said.

"No one has," Lyra checked her coat for burn

marks. *"If they risked sending a firemental, things must be bad."*

There was concern in Storm's golden eyes. *"The situation on Aldenmor must be worsening."*

Emily said, "What do we do now?"

"Should we contact Zach?" Adriane asked. Zach lived on Aldenmor and would know how bad things had gotten. Adriane was worried about him and the mistwolves.

"What good would that do?" Kara said, suddenly aware of how much she hated feeling helpless and scared.

"If we're going to save Aldenmor, we've got to stop talking about it and *do* it!" She tossed her golden hair over a shoulder, forging ahead before she could stop to think about what she was saying. "The firemental came for us!" Kara said sternly.

The room was silent. They all knew Kara was right. The time had come for the girls to put all they had learned to the test. To act now. Or it would be too late.

"There *is* only one way to find out what Kara did to the portals," Adriane said.

"We have to use the unicorn horn and open the portal here on Ravenswood," Kara said. "Just like I did before."

"And go through it wherever it leads," Emily added.

"The fairimentals sent me to find you," Ozzie said sadly. "It's time to bring you back."

"Time to save our friends," Storm said.

Lyra pushed her large head into Kara's side. *"We stand together."*

"We'll bring the unicorn horn and the fairy map," Kara said, racing ahead before she could change her mind. "The magic of the horn should keep us safe."

"I'll tell Gran we're going on a school trip," Adriane said.

"I'll get the Pet Palace shut down," Emily said.

"I'll go pack," Kara concluded firmly.

Everyone looked at Kara.

"What?" the blond-haired girl said demurely. "I'm not going without a change of clothes!"

"Good to have you back, Kara," Emily smiled.

Kara grinned and glanced at Adriane.

The dark-haired girl raised her fist and touched Kara's fist. "Okay, we'll meet at the portal field in half an hour."

"What should we tell the others?" asked Ronif.

"Tell them to get ready!" Kara said. "We're going to bring them home."

Chapter 3

T he noon sun broke through patchwork clouds as animals filled the large, open field in the north quadrant of the wildlife preserve. It was here they had first appeared in Ravenswood — wommels, brimbees, pegasi, jeeran, and all the others, desperately rushing through the hidden doorway from their world to be healed.

The surrounding forest was already thinning as maples and oaks offered their final gift of colors. Soon they would submit to their cold slumber. Only the never-changing green of the pines would tough it out until spring.

Emily, Adriane, Kara, Lyra, Storm, and Ozzie made their way through the throng of adoring, cheering creatures. Rasha, Ronif, and Balthazar followed, setting off another round of hoots, hollers, neighs, and chirps. Word had spread fast that the girls had been called by the firemental. The ancient prophecy was about to be fulfilled.

Three young mages and their magical animal friends were going to save their world.

Ozzie spoke first.

"When I first met the fairimentals," he began, "they told me I would play a part in fighting dark magic and saving our world. I'm a ferr — an elf! I didn't believe it possible. Now, I'm here to tell you I believe!" The ferret raised his furry arms dramatically as the crowd reacted with more cheers.

"I believe in our friends and I believe in the magic." Ozzie began shuffling back and forth, calling out to the crowd. "And with a little luck, you'll all see home again." Dramatically, he fell to one knee, arms outstretched. "You just have to believe!"

More cheers met Ozzie's impassioned speech. They all needed to hear those words. Uncertainties lay ahead. The girls knew it. Their journey together had been as unpredictable as it had been rewarding. Yet each knew one thing for sure — something the fairimentals had told them: *There is no going back.*

Did they really believe they could do what they were chosen for?

Emily thought about how far she'd come, only to now stand at the crossroads between science and faith. Her first magical friend, Phel, had taught her healing was more than knowledge of medicine and technique, it was rooted deep in compassion and empathy. What would she believe when her faith was put to the test?

Adriane looked at her amber wolfstone set in the onyx and turquoise band on her wrist. The silver mistwolf beside her matched the reflective stripes down the sides of Adriane's black track pants.

Her grandmother called Adriane "Little Bird," an homage to their Indian heritage. Headstrong, Adriane had always fought with an iron will, barreling forward in a straight line, determined to find her own name, her own place. Thanks to Stormbringer, she knew she was not just a fighter, but a warrior with courage to soar free like a . . . bird. She smiled. No, to run free like a wolf. She was bonded forever with the mistwolves and Stormbringer.

"Little Wolf," Storm said, looking at her with deep golden eyes.

With Storm at her side, Adriane could do anything.

"All right, Ronif, Rasha, Balthazar, you're in charge now," Emily said. "Just try to keep everyone's spirits up."

"We will do our best," Balthazar said.

"As soon as the portal opens, call to Moonshadow and Silver Eyes," Adriane told Storm. "See if you can get a reading on what's going on over there."

"I will try." Storm remained ever calm, ever strong.

"I think I have everything," Kara said, brushing her long blond hair back while rummaging in her backpack. Lyra stood beside her friend, grooming her own lustrous spotted fur. Kara was wearing designer hiking boots, dark denim jeans, and a faux fur-trimmed safari coat. Slung over her shoulder was a bright red backpack.

Kara was beginning to understand that her journey was tied to the magic more than anyone had thought possible. She was the conductor. Without her, magic had little focus, no direction. With her, magic shone in endless circles, spreading like the golden radiance of her smile. It had a profound effect on everyone — human and animal — she came into contact with. But just as still waters ran deep, she felt something more, a darkness just below the surface, waiting to drag her down.

"Kara, you have the fairy map?" Emily asked.

"Fairy map, check." She lifted the glowing ball from her pack. Tiny star patterns sparkled inside, a mysterious key to the pathways of the web.

Everyone looked with awe upon the gift given to Kara by the fairimentals. With this map, Kara had opened pathways of portals to parts unknown on the magic web.

"Unicorn horn?" Adriane asked.

"Right here," Kara held up the horn. Sunlight split the crystal, and a thousand sparkles raced up and down the swirled horn.

"Kara, what else is in there?" Emily asked, curiously eyeing her bulging backpack.

"Just some essentials," Kara replied. "Granola bars, a toothbrush, hairspray, Breath Blast, hair clips, a change of socks, some lip balms, chips. . . ."

"Where do you think we're going? Paris?" Adriane asked.

"Well, we don't really know, do we?" Kara shot back.

"Let's find out," Emily said.

Kara held the unicorn horn up high.

The crowd fanned out to a wide circle giving the young mages room.

The three girls stood close together, Ozzie before them, Lyra and Storm on either side.

Slowly, Adriane reached out and grasped Kara's hand, wrapping her fingers around it and the unicorn horn. Adriane's wolf stone glinted, then glowed bright gold.

Then Emily reached out, adding her hand to the others. Her rainbow jewel began to glow, pulsing blue-green light.

The crowd fell silent as spirals of amber and blue-green magic raced from the jewels swirling around the girls' arms. They could feel the animals in the field adding their own individual strength of will, helping to focus the magic.

"Okay, here we go." Kara pushed fear from her mind as she felt the magic surging though her. She recognized it and opened herself as it built, rising into waves of power, using her as a vehicle for its release. She focused and bent the power to her will.

"Concentrate on the dreamcatcher," Emily said, closing her eyes. "Picture it opening!"

A hidden, magical dreamcatcher protected the portal. It was constructed from strands of the magic web itself. One thing the girls had learned was that magic attracts magic. Power surged from Adriane's and Emily's jewels and flowed through Kara, around her body, up her arms, and right into the horn of the unicorn. A stream of magic fire burst from the horn, skyrocketing into the sky.

"Hold it steady!" Adriane yelled.

Kara whirled the beam of crystal starlight in a giant circle slicing the air with twinkles. The dreamcatcher appeared before them, hanging in the air just above the ground. Its circular center widened, revealing a curtain of mist. It was through this opening they'd have to go.

Lightning sparked even though there was no sign of a storm. The meadow below them suddenly lurched as the air seemed to twist. Thunder rolled and the sky cracked, splitting open the dark void. Winking stars that seemed to sit on glowing lines stretched behind the dreamcatcher. Although the girls had seen it before, looking into the yawning void was breathtaking. The magic web was incredible, at once beautiful and awesome, and, as they well knew, incredibly dangerous.

Emily drew in a breath. "Here we go," she murmured.

"Stay close together. Concentrate on forming a single protective bubble so we don't get separated," Emily instructed. Ozzie scampered up her leg to sit upon her shoulder.

"Okay." Adriane stood strong, holding onto Storm's neck.

The magic swirled, dancing faster around them. Gold, blue, and silver lit the field with dazzling brightness.

The center of the dreamcatcher opened wider before them.

"One jumps —" Adriane said.

"We all jump!" Kara finished.

And with that, Emily, Adriane, Kara, Ozzie, Lyra, and Storm leaped through the dreamcatcher into the portal beyond.

"Emily!" Ozzie cried, grasping Emily's neck.

"I've got you," Emily shouted back.

Triggered by the immense power of the web,

magic flew from Emily's rainbow jewel, Adriane's wolf stone, and the unicorn horn held by Kara. At once, an amber bubble covered in crackling blue light encircled them.

The bubble floated above the strands of stars like a giant balloon.

Emily quickly took count to make sure they were all still together. "It's okay, Ozzie. You can open your eyes."

The ferret open one eye and gazed through the translucent bubble at the endless spirals of web.

"Gah!"

The bubble quickly picked up speed as it slid between stands of golden lines. They were traveling toward a sequence of portals, winking in the distance.

"We're on the web," Adriane said.

"It's awesome!" Ozzie exclaimed.

The orb dropped onto another tier of golden strands. The web spread out before them like a galaxy. Pinpoints sparkled, but it was impossible to tell how far away the stars were — or how close.

"Are you getting anything, Storm?" Emily asked.

"When I jumped through before, it took me right to Aldenmor," Storm answered.

"Same here," Adriane added.

"And that's how all the animals came through," Emily reminded them.

"So why aren't we going to Aldenmor?" Kara asked.

"Because Kara's spellsinging changed the pathway," Ozzie realized.

"There's something else," Storm said. *"Something has happened to Moonshadow."*

"What?" Adriane asked worriedly.

"I can't get a clear picture. The mistwolves wait for us at Mount Hope."

"So where are we going?" Kara asked.

"What I wouldn't give for a flobbin right now!" Ozzie commented, remembering the magic tracking creature.

"I thought the unicorns were fixing the web," Kara pointed out as the bubble sped past sections of web — broken, hanging, and tangled.

"Stay away from the broken strands," Emily called out.

Adriane raised her wolf stone, guiding the bubble along the path.

Emily pointed to the unicorn horn in Kara's hand. The crystal pulsed with brilliant light. "Lorelei's horn," Emily said. "Remember what she told us. We can use the magic of the unicorn. It was given to us."

Emily thought of her magical friend. Unicorns ran along the strands of the web itself, repairing it so magic could flow where it was supposed to go.

But here strands were horribly distorted, broken, and sparking like downed electrical cables. How could the unicorns hope to repair such immense damage?

The girls once again held hands as Kara raised the horn.

"Lorelei! Take us to where we're supposed to go!" Emily called out.

Instantly, the bubble took a sharp dip, spiraling into a sweeping curve, right toward a knot of broken, tangled strands. The knot sparked dangerously ahead.

"Not that way!" Ozzie yelled, trying to push the bubble in the opposite direction.

"Hang on!" Adriane shouted.

"To what?"

FLASH.

Dead silence.

For a split second, everyone was silhouetted in a blaze of white — then the web appeared, hurtling around them as they shot from the open portal.

Stars became streaks as the orb careened down layers of strands.

Adriane held onto the fur of Storm's neck as the bubble twisted, picking up more speed. Its thin walls were beginning to stretch, sizzling with power.

"Keep focused!" Kara shouted. "Hold it together!"

The bubble spun violently, dropped like a runaway roller coaster and — *FLASH* — rocketed though another portal like a meteor.

Emily lost her grip and was thrown against the thin walls of the bubble. Electricity sparked from her jewel, sending fire racing around the orb. She reached out and snatched Ozzie's leg before he bounced away.

Kara and Lyra were flattened against the other side. Electrical energy flashed and crackled along the bubble.

Kara felt her hand push right through the wall! Their protective shell was not going to hold together much longer.

"It's breaking up," Kara yelled. Wind whipped around them, sounding like a tornado. "We've got to stay together!"

Emily and Adriane strained forward, reaching to grasp hands, but the forces holding them apart were too strong.

"Something's coming up and fast!" Ozzie screamed, falling over Emily's head.

Ahead of them, a tight cluster of shimmering stars was getting bigger by the second.

"It's a nexus!" Emily called out.

The nexus hung like a thickly woven platform of light. Surrounding it were high walls that held dozens of portals. Here, strands of the web interconnected, each portal leading to a different destination.

"Try to stay together!" Adriane commanded.

"As long as we stay together, we'll be okay," Emily called, hand outstretched, trying to inch her way toward Adriane.

"We're coming in too fast!" Ozzie screamed.

"We're going to hit," Emily yelled.

The bubble careened toward the nexus floor and spun out of control.

"Ahhh!"

Adriane clung to Storm. Ozzie buried his head into Emily's neck. Lyra's magical wings flared open to protect Kara.

The bubble hit hard, bouncing into the air, coming down again, skidding and rolling. With a sudden blast of twinkling lights, the protective orb exploded apart and vanished.

They were all thrown in different directions.

"Emily!"

"Adriane!"

Instantly, a blue-green bubble formed around Emily and Ozzie.

An amber bubble formed around Adriane and Storm.

Silver diamond power blazed from the horn in Kara's hand, wrapping her and Lyra in a crystal cocoon.

The bubbles smashed into the walls of the nexus and vanished, swallowed into three different portals.

Chapter 4

Wind whipped waves of white, wrapping Adriane in cold. She covered her face, trying to see through the blizzard, thankful she had worn a down vest and heavy sweater.

"Storm?" She called out, suddenly afraid her friend had landed some place far from her.

"*I am here,*" the wolf called out.

Adriane turned at the sound of the voice in her head. She instantly felt better. That connection, no matter how far away, was always a part of her.

She pulled her wool hat tight over her ears and trudged, head low, through the heavy snow. Within seconds, she found Storm. Dropping to her knees, she hugged the wolf close. "Thank goodness you're okay. I can't see a thing!"

"*We have to get out of the storm.*"

"Can you sense the others?" Adriane asked hopefully.

"*No.*"

"What about the portal we fell through?"

"There's nothing here now. We have to move. I sense danger."

Adriane quickly turned, trying to see through the blinding storm. "Which way?"

"We must move toward the mountains."

"Okay. Let's go." She got to her feet, and pulled the cuff of her sweater up to expose the wolf stone on her wrist. She concentrated. Instantly, the stone flared to light, casting a golden glow against the haze of ice and snow. The pair moved as fast as they could through the wall of white.

"Are we on Aldenmor?" Adriane tried to ignore the sharp cold hammering down.

"Yes."

"Okay, well at least we're here . . . wherever that is."

"Somewhere in the northern coastal region."

"How do you know that?"

"I can smell brine of the ocean mixed in the wind. The storm is passing over."

Her mistwolf senses were sharp. Sure enough, it wasn't long before the blizzard began to trail away. The fog separated, and the vista in front of them was breathtaking. Towering glacier-covered mountains rose from the rolling tundra, bordered by huge brown cliffs.

Sounds seeped through the wind. Soaring gulls skimmed the dunes that ran not fifty yards from where they stood.

Adriane turned in a slow circle hoping to catch a glimpse of Emily, Kara, Lyra, or even Ozzie. She scanned the wide plateau they had crossed, but all she saw was stark white landscape whipped by cold winds.

"Are we still in danger?"

"Yes. Something is hunting."

Adriane bit her lower lip. She'd been hunted once before on Aldenmor. Creatures had used her magic jewel like a LoJack to track her. Quickly, she covered the bracelet with her sleeve.

"Can you reach the mistwolves?" she asked Storm.

The mistwolf looked out beyond the giant ice mountains and closed her eyes. Adriane strained to hear a response from the wolfpack, but only the wind echoed in her ears.

"Help!"

Adriane whipped her head around.

Storm's ears pricked up. *"The hunters have found prey."*

"Where?"

Storm nodded toward the dunes.

Adriane focused.

"Help us!"

The call came again, this time more frantic. And then another sound. The unmistakable cry of an animal in pain.

Adriane and Storm took off toward the cry. The icy ground was slippery, but they were swift and sure. They covered the open snowy ground quickly, carefully picking their way up the rock-strewn dunes. Adriane crouched and eased herself toward the crest — she looked over.

She caught a quick glimpse of rocky beach and ice-covered water before *the thing* was on her!

It leaped from the far side, a wave of fur and teeth, roaring like a hurricane. Startled, Adriane fell back, tripping over loose shale and coral. It was the fall that saved her as a razor-clawed paw swept the air where she had been a second before. Big as a bear with piercing eyes black as coal, the snow creature stood on massive hind legs, its matted white fur thick with congealed mud and dirt. Adriane rolled into a fighting stance. Suddenly, the creature vanished, toppled over the dune by a roaring rush of silver-furred fury.

Adriane jumped over the dune and skidded to the bottom. The snow creature rolled across the stone-covered beach, attempting to remove the mistwolf from its back.

"Storm!"

Three other snow monsters turned at once,

looking up from the shallow waters of the wide bay. They were using their sharp, long claws to drag a large sea creature out of the waves and onto the frozen shore. Hazy sun reflected off emerald scales as the huge animal thrashed in the shallow water. It was the size of a whale but much sleeker, with tremendous flippers that it used to slap at its attackers. Gills along its sinewy neck opened and closed, fanning desperately for air. A long slash just below its dorsal leaked fluid into the crystal-blue waters, white with froth and red with blood.

Confident their prey was sufficiently wounded, the snow monsters abandoned the scaled sea beast and moved toward the dunes.

Adriane chanced a quick look up the beach and saw the first attacker lying motionless. Storm was nowhere to be seen. With a roar, the monsters raced toward Adriane.

"I think I got their attention," she whispered, sweeping her right arm into the air. Her damp sweater fell away exposing the wolf stone wild with bright amber light.

The creatures slowed at the sight, then fanned out to box in the intruder.

Locking into a fighting stance, Adriane felt the fire building along her arm, waiting to be let loose.

She eyed the bear creatures, choosing the biggest and most dangerous. She settled on the one in the middle, a huge mass of fur and teeth. She'd take him out first.

Magic fire flew from her jewel and whipped out in a golden ring. Instantly, the ring circled the giant bear. The creature leaped back in fright, trying to rip away the fire. The others skidded to a stop, unsure how to deal with this new situation.

Adriane stepped forward, whipping concentric rings of fire into the air, trying her best to make a fearsome display. Before the creatures could decide what to do, a terrifying growl erupted behind them — a silver mistwolf. Lips pulled back to reveal fierce teeth, ears flat, Storm was ready to spring.

The bear creatures decided to abandon their prey for the moment, slinking down the beach, then moving behind the dunes.

Adriane turned to the sea creature they'd attacked. During the fight, it must have managed to work itself into the surf. With a final painful cry and what looked like a wave of its flipper, it dove beneath the waves.

Adriane and Storm stood together on the windswept shore. Before them was a vast ocean strewn with ice. It stretched as far as the eye could see. Waves tipped with froth churned against the large ice flows.

"We surprised them, but they'll be back," Storm said, catching the worry in Adriane's dark eyes.

"What do we do?"

"We have to get to Mount Hope," Storm answered.

"Suggestions?"

"It's a long trek."

Suddenly, geysers of water erupted offshore. With gruff snorts, four sea creatures broke the surface. Giant green dragonlike heads with large slitted golden eyes stared at the girl and wolf. But Adriane's gaze was drawn to what sat upon their backs. Green-skinned with long flowing kelplike hair, they stared at Adriane and Storm.

"You there!" A young man called out from the back of his sea dragon. He looked to be sixteen or seventeen, but it was hard to tell.

"Who are you? What are you doing here?" Adriane asked, astonished.

"Waiting," he answered.

"For what?"

"You."

❀   ❀   ❀

"Here, try this." Ozzie emerged from the thick bushes, and handed Emily a paw full of red berries. "Bubbleberries. Should settle your tummy."

"How do you know they're safe to eat?" Uncertainly, Emily looked at the small berries in her hands.

"Spoof!" Ozzie spit out a slew of berries. "Quick! Is my tongue green?" He stuck out a red tongue.

"No."

"Good. Then they're okay." He went back to stuffing his mouth. "I used to pick these all the time when I was younger. They grow all over the Moorgroves."

Broken sunlight dappled through boughs of tall treetops. Emily and Ozzie walked along a wide road they'd discovered soon after arriving in the forest lands. Ozzie was sure they were in the Moorgroves, a dense forest region covering an immense area of Aldenmor. Even though the sun shone overhead, they could see twin moons, Della and Orpheus, rising just above the horizon.

"If we stay on the road, we'll end up somewhere," Ozzie said, munching away. "Arahoo Wells, Dumble Downs, Billicontwee. I was going to visit my cousins, Crusp and Tonin, in Dumble Downs that night I ran into the fairimentals."

"Is the Fairy Glen somewhere in the Moorgroves?" Emily asked.

"Could be. There's a portal somewhere near Dream Lake, I remember that."

No one had heard from the fairimentals for weeks until that firemental had come for the girls.

"As long as we don't wander into the Misty Marshes, we should be okay," Ozzie said, looking worriedly up at Emily. "How are you feeling?"

"Better," Emily answered bravely, rubbing at

her wrist. As soon as they had arrived in the thick forests, she knew something wasn't right. Dancing shadows moved across the road, making her feel dizzy and feverish. Her clothes clung, heavy with sweat, her mind seemed thick and foggy. And her stomach churned, threatening to empty her breakfast upon the trail.

Trying to keep focused, she asked, "So you really grew up near here?"

"The Moorgroves border Elf country. My village of Farthingdale is on the eastern Grassy Plains in the most beautiful rolling hills full of wildflowers. Wait till you see!"

"But we haven't seen anyone since we started on this road," Emily said, observing patches of open hills through the forests as they walked.

Shadows skimmed the ground fading into the woods.

"We're sure to spot someone, and they can tell us how to find someone who knows someone who knows how to get to Mount Hope —"

Ozzie looked behind him. Emily had stopped, rubbing at her wrist.

"What?" Ozzie asked, suddenly aware he'd been talking to himself.

"I don't know. Something doesn't feel right."

Ozzie ran back. "Let's have a look."

Emily pulled up the sleeve of her cardigan

sweater. Deep red and purple light burst from the rainbow jewel, erratically pulsing like a dull heartbeat.

Ozzie's eyes widened. "That doesn't look right at all."

"It's hurting me, Ozzie!" Emily said, rubbing the jewel harder, willing the itching burn to stop.

But the jewel only pulsed darker, deep purples swirling to green and black.

Emily felt the darkness infecting her jewel. She tried to focus. Think. When had she felt these strange, sickening feelings before? Suddenly, she remembered —

"Emily!"

Ozzie's scream broke her concentration. She saw the ferret yanking at her jeans, trying to pull her from the open road.

A dark shadow passed overhead. Emily raised her jewel to cover her eyes as she looked up. Something huge blotted the brightness. It looked like a giant bat, glistening black wings swept behind a sleek head. It had a short hooked beak and red flashing eyes. On its back, a gruesome figure rode, apelike and covered in rough armor of leather and steel. It held a crooked staff of polished metal tipped with a red crystal. A wedge of sharp teeth formed a grin as it bore down on the flying beast.

"Run!"

Emily saw the ferret hopping up and down, gesturing wildly.

She willed her legs to move off the road and into the cool darkness of shadows. Dust and dirt flew in her face from the sharp beating of wings.

"Run, Emily!" Ozzie screamed again.

The dark rider skimmed above Emily's head, almost knocking her to the ground. The crystal upon its staff flared like a demon sun. Ground, grass, and rock exploded, sending Emily flying past a tree. Coughing and choking, she propped herself on her elbows, trying to find Ozzie.

"Over here!" the ferret whispered as loud as he could.

Emily quickly crawled over a grassy mound and fell behind a wide, narrow knoll, thick with moss.

Shadows circled overhead, dark shapes breaking above the open treetops.

"What are they, Ozzie?" Emily was breathing hard, pulling twigs from her curly red hair as she hunkered half buried in deep ferns.

"Goblin riders. This is bad. What are they doing in the Moorgroves — *oh, no!*"

Emily capped her hand over the ferret's mouth. "Shhhh!"

"*Garg* — don't you understand?" the ferret asked, pushing her hand away. "The fairimentals

48

have protected this part of Aldenmor for years. Now that they're gone — everyone here is in danger!"

"Where should we go?"

"We can't stay here. We have to find the elves!"

Emily's jewel had cooled to a dim glow but still swirled with maroon and black.

She was a healer. But could she heal herself?

She closed her eyes, willing herself to cleanse the jewel. To feel something clean, pure, and good — but all she felt was the familiar sickening poison, seeping with darkness.

"Ozzie, I feel something."

"What?"

"It's . . . I think . . . maybe . . . it's —"

"What, what?!"

"Black Fire," she said finally.

"*Gah!* Where?"

"Not far. Over that way." Emily pointed toward a thicket of forest.

Ozzie was on his feet pulling at her arm. "Can you make it?"

"I think so."

"Let's go!"

They scampered through the undergrowth, carefully picking their way over logs, fallen trees, rocks, and brush.

With an eye to the skies for any sign of the goblin riders, they quickly made their way to a hillside that sloped into a valley of green beyond.

"How close are we to your home?" Emily asked, worriedly.

"That's the Grassy Plains. Not far."

They didn't have to say what they really feared. If Black Fire had spread beyond the dark circle of the Shadowlands, Aldenmor was in terrible danger.

Distracted by her thoughts, Emily didn't see the edge where most of the forest floor had eroded.

"Look out!" Ozzie shouted as Emily set her foot down.

Emily tried to grab onto a thin sapling — but her foot slipped. Chunks of wet dirt fell away as her body hit the ground. She rolled and tumbled down the incline before coming to stop at the bottom of a wide gully. Arms out, splayed flat, Emily steadied herself and gingerly pushed to her knees.

She sensed them before she saw them. About a dozen small creatures surrounding her, each standing about four feet tall, wearing boots of tanned leather, woolen pants and leather shirts and vests. Each carried a long, sharp spear, pointed directly at her. She looked to see their faces and gasped. Their heads were contorted and gruesome, snarling, and heavily adorned with war paint.

Pink.

That's pretty, Kara thought, walking upon golden grass soft as rabbit fur through swirling mists of pinks, yellows, greens, and purples. She didn't feel scared. In fact, she felt strangely happy, almost giddy.

"Where do you think we are, Lyra?" she asked the large cat close by her side.

"I don't know," Lyra replied. *"But we're sure not on Aldenmor."*

> *There's magic in the air*
> *Love is everywhere*
> *All our friends are gathered 'round*
> *To celebrate the fair*

Singing! Someone's singing.

"Over that way," Lyra said, sensing Kara's thoughts.

An expanse of forest wild with oak and ivy became visible as the pinks and yellows thinned. Excited voices became clear, cheering, whooping and giggling.

"Sounds like someone's having a party!" Kara said, looking at multicolored lights flashing in the distance.

Come and join the fun
Dancing under the sun
Let's wave our hands
To all our fans
The party's just begun

"Can you feel it, feel the magic." Kara was humming along to the catchy song, skipping light as air as she danced through the mist and into the full-blown fairy rave!

Feel the magic
Can you feel it
Feel the magic
Everyone can't help but sing along

The music pounded, loud and strong, sending infectious sounds soaring over the enchanted gardens.

"Whoa!" Kara raised her arms, swaying to the beat.

Even the magic glade at Ravenswood couldn't hold a candle to this place — wherever she was. Explosions of color seemed to burst from everywhere. Fragrant, buttery yellow flowers, each painted with bright red stars hung like trees over the main party area. Long spears of heather, turquoise and golden, swayed to the rhythms. Violet primrose and garlands of silver birch glittered over rings of toadstools.

The music blasted from a stage set upon a circle of tumbled stones at the far end of the immense garden where three performers played.

The air bristled as rainbow sparkles cascaded gently, making everyone twinkle and glitter. And the place was jammed, teeming with all kinds of magical creatures Kara had never seen before.

"Fairy rave," Lyra said with disgust. *"Don't get too close. The magic is intoxicating. They'll lure you —* Kara?" Lyra looked around for her missing blond friend.

Kara danced by shimmying big-footed kobolds. She shook and hopped past cute little brownies and hooting hobgoblins. She bopped and boogied with five raucous long-bearded gnomes. Somewhere in the back of her mind a nagging thought told her she didn't have time for this. She should be looking for someone, Kara thought. Some friends. They were supposed to be doing something important, only she couldn't remember exactly what it was. And at the moment, it didn't seem all that urgent. All she wanted to do was rock out to the music.

> *I looked up to the skies*
> *And much to my surprise*
> *Things are changing right before my eyes*

You got to follow every dream
'Cause your time is coming soon

"Kara!" Lyra called, slinking through the silky, hypnotic rhythm of the music, paws firmly on the ground.

Pint-sized purple pixies perched on purled fronds. Fat big-eyed bogles tossed toadstools and drank from thimble-sized cups on the huge lawn. Spriggles and sproggins huddled under tables gobbling strange-looking foods. Leprechauns wandered around knocking into one another belly first and hooting hysterically. And darting over all of them, perching on blooms and dancing in circles were vibrant, luminous beings, beautiful gossamer-winged fairies!

> *Feel the magic*
> *Can you feel it*
> *Feel the magic*
> *Everyone can't help but sing along*

Kara was in the center of the party, all kinds of creatures were dancing around her.

Then she saw three performers onstage. They were totally kickin' it. The band was human-sized, like her. The lead singer's long raven hair flowed as she moved and twirled, scarves billowing around her like silk clouds.

With hair of neon pink and flaming red, the drummer leaped and jumped, pounding out the rhythm on anything she could find — including the heads of two overzealous bridge trolls!

Golden-skinned with dark blue hair, the guitar player hammered a strange-looking instrument of burnished wood that flared and glowed under her amazingly talented fingers.

"Woooo!! They totally rock!" Kara yelled, waving her arms, moving to the beat. The music was glorious, filling the garden with the most incredible magic. It was as if nothing else mattered, nothing else felt this good.

Kara danced with a pointy-toed, top-hatted, purple spriggle. The fairy creature raised his feet and arms, dancing up a storm.

"I'm Kara, what's your name?" Kara giggled, giving the pint-sized fairy her best smile.

"Me name?!" the fairy creature said, abruptly coming to a stop. "Why, I'll wark ye muckle tarrie!"

"Okaaaay." Kara danced away and into a cloud of sparkling wings.

"Ya poof git!" the angry fairy yelled, waving his small fist at her.

Beautiful silver- and blue-winged fairies converged about her, lifting her hair, tickling her arms and legs. A few beady-eyed hobgoblins dropped into the fray struggling with Kara's backpack. Snickering and hooting, they opened the zipper, diving in and rifling through the treasures.

One pulled out a granola bar. "Ye moog haggle!"

"Gimme, ya booty bogger!" Another cried.

They struggled over the power bar, falling to the ground as another pulled out an orange sock, which he promptly put over his head. "Farf doodle!"

Kara was surrounded by fairy creatures, converging all over her.

"Git, yer pookin muckle!"

There was a loud commotion behind her.

The fairy map — it floated out of the backpack! Sparkling stars winked and blinked inside the orb. A dozen spriggles had piled up on top of one another, trying to grab it, but the orb floated out of their reach. It rose into the air and hovered above the excited crowd.

"Hey, that's mine!" Kara said, easily grabbing the blue orb back into her arms.

The music came to an abrupt halt.

Everyone stopped dancing, frozen, staring at Kara with wide eyes and dropped jaws.

"The magic is with you."

She spun around to the stage. The band was staring at Kara.

"What?" Kara checked her clothes. "Did I get any on me?"

The flaming-haired drummer leaped from the stage, landing gracefully at Kara's feet in a deep bow. "We've awaited your return, Princess."

The entire crowd fell to the ground, bowing profusely and groveling at Kara's feet.

"What gives? Who are you?" Kara asked the pointy-eared fairy musicians.

"We are spellsingers," the silky siren singer said.

The drummer jumped to her feet, tapping a fast rhythm with her boots, "Maybe you've heard of us. We're Be*Tween."

Chapter 5

Icy blue waters rolled past the sleek sea dragon as it sped along the surface, leaving a wake of froth in its trail. Powerful fins and a long tail skimming like a rudder kept the riders on its back steady and sure. Adriane and Storm sat in front of the sleek dorsal fin. They watched the green-skinned boy from the sea talk to his mount as he sat astride its wide neck, gently stroking tapered fins behind the beast's wide, scaled head. It made Adriane think of Zachariah and the way he had been with Windy, his brave Griffin friend.

The merboy's clothes were sea-green and blue, like a diver's wetsuit. Around his neck hung an opalescent star-shaped jewel. His long green hair was pulled back and tied with several cords draped with shells. Pointy ears peeked from his kelplike hair.

"How did you know we would be here?" Adriane asked the boy, whose name was Jaaran. "We were told you would come," Jaaran explained.

Adriane noticed the boy's eyes had two sets of lids. She guessed one was for protection underwater. He had wide webbing between his fingers, and his bare feet formed natural fins of webbed toes.

"Told by whom?" Adriane asked.

"The mistwolves."

Before she could react, the sea erupted. Geysers of water spiraled high into the air around them. Adriane and Storm watched, astonished, as several sea dragons leaped, arcing high into the air and gracefully diving nose-first back into the water. They were amazing creatures. And atop each rode a merboy or mergirl! One sea dragon cut through the rolling ocean currents, swimming alongside Adriane and Storm. It snorted and opened translucent lids revealing large golden eyes.

On its back sat a girl, long green hair flowing in the wind. Like the merboy, she had webbed fingers and toes. A sea-green shell sparkled around her neck. "Meerka sends her thanks to you. As do I, Mage," she said. Her webbed fingers formed a fist and tapped it to her chest.

Adriane noticed the ragged wounds along the creature's side. This was the one they had saved from the snow monsters.

"I am Kee-Lyn," the mergirl said, pulling Meerka close alongside. "The beasts caught us off guard and attacked." Her voice lilted like waves lapping on the shore. "They are not from this realm of Aldenmor. They appeared out of nowhere."

"I know the feeling," Adriane said. She added, "I'm Adriane and this is Storm."

Jaaran nodded. "The magic of Aldenmor runs wild."

"Is Meerka all right?" Adriane asked.

Kee-Lyn hunched forward, hugging her sea dragon's thick scaled neck. "If not for you, Meerka would have been killed. The sea heals her now."

"When did the mistwolves call to you?" Storm asked.

"When did you hear from them last?" Adriane added anxiously.

"Two days ago. The pack leader told us you would come to bring the rain of lights."

"Rain of lights?" Adriane asked Storm.

"The lights may be a reaction to the portals Kara opened with her spellsinging," Storm mused.

"How magnificent to bond with a mistwolf," the mergirl said with reverence and awe.

Adriane nodded. "Stormbringer and I are from Earth. We both run with the pack."

"The sea dragons and mistwolves run the same path." Jaaran told them.

"How so?" Storm asked.

"Once long ago, there were thousands of sea dragons as there were mistwolves. Not anymore."

"The Dark Sorceress hunts them for their magic," Kee-lyn explained, her ocean-blue eyes full of grief.

Adriane understood. "I have been in the witch's lair. I know she covets the magic of such great creatures."

The riders looked at one another, astonished.

"You escaped the dark circle?" Jaaran asked.

"With the help of the pack and a boy named Zach," Adriane explained. "I thought there were no other humans on Aldenmor . . . until I met Zach."

"We are descended from humans thousands of years ago," Jaaran said, "but our home now is in the great oceans with the sea dragons."

It was Adriane's turn to look astonished.

Human? How could this be possible?

"But the magic of Aldenmor grows weaker each day. And with it so does the race of merfolk," Jaaran added.

"You also wear jewels. They must hold magic," Adriane observed.

"These are the Jewels of the Sea, designated to the chosen riders. We are the select few chosen to ride with the dragons to protect our world."

"And one day we, too, shall be mages, friend!" Kee-lyn added.

"I am honored to be called friend by you, but I am not a mage." Adriane told them.

Meerka snorted, turning deep, golden eyes on Adriane. *"You fight well. The magic is with you."*

Adriane stared into the deep eyes.

"She is a warrior," Storm said.

Satisfied, Meerka turned back to the sea. *"When the lights appear, magic will rain."*

Magic rain?

"Will it be dark or light rain that falls?" Kee-Lyn asked.

"The time is at hand, and we stand ready to fight or die with our world," Jaaran said.

"How do you know all this?" Adriane was awed.

"It was the last message from the fairimentals before they vanished," Jaaran said.

The fairimentals! "Do you know what's happened to them?"

Kee-Lyn's face fell. "We fear for them," she said sadly. "We fear the Dark Sorceress has broken their magic. Soon the seas will suffer the same fate."

"You said you know a portal that can take us to Mount Hope. Is that portal still safe?" Adriane asked, hugging herself to keep warm.

Jaaran said, "The pack leader wore a fairy map. He told us the portal remains true."

Adriane smiled inwardly. She had given the fairy map to Moonshadow as a gift from the fairimentals. "Where is this portal?" she asked.

The sea dragon came to a stop, gently bobbing on the open sea.

"Here," Jaaran spoke.

Adriane looked around, confused. All she saw was open water. Large ice flows drifted in the distance, and beyond a stark coastline, spotted with browns and greens.

With a snort, Leeka pointed his great head into the waters.

"The coral forest, below," Jaaran explained.

Leaning slightly to the side, Adriane rested her head on Storm's soft silver fur and drew strength from the mistwolf. Squeezing Storm's flank lightly, Adriane straightened, stood, and took a deep breath. Whatever grand scheme was unfolding, she and her friends had a destiny to fulfill.

Ready or not, they would fight for this world.

She raised her jewel and concentrated. The wolf stone blazed to life with an amber glow. There *was* strong magic here.

"You will lead us there?" Adriane asked.

"Yes," Kee-Lyn answered.

Adriane rolled back her sleeve and focused on her wolf stone. The amber stone grew warm and began to shimmer. When the shimmer became a broad arc of light, Adriane waved her arm, forming a circle of light. Storm pressed close to her, and the circle slowly surrounded them, sealing itself closed.

"We're ready," Adriane said.

Kee-Lyn looked into Adriane's eyes and nodded. "The magic is with you."

Meerka rolled her body forward in a smooth motion, and suddenly Adriane was watching the surface light fall away like a hazy dream.

Adriane focused hard on her stone, keeping the bubble protectively closed.

They sank fast, watching a thousand bubbles circle around them.

Below, the immense forest of coral revealed itself, like a jungle across the sea floor.

They dove below towering reefs of vivid colors, oranges, reds, purples, and blues. And the sea teemed with a cornucopia of colorful fish, plants, and sea creatures unlike Adriane had ever seen — or imagined. Schools of large sea horses swam through swaying kelp curiously watching the dragons and the strange creatures inside the magical globe.

"Kelpies," Storm observed, her golden eyes focused intently on the bubble wall. *"Sea horses."*

"It's incredible," Adriane was overwhelmed by the magnificent beauty. Would there be enough time to save it all from disappearing?

At the base of the reef, the sea dragons banked under a coral bridge and arrived at a giant underwater cave.

"This is it," Kee-Lyn said. "The portal is just on the other side of the mouth of the cave."

"Thank you," Adriane said. "I hope we will meet again."

"As do we, Warrior Mage Adriane," Meerka said.

"We pledge ourselves to your service, Mage," Kee-Lyn said.

Adriane lowered her arm, and the bubble moved forward, lightly floating from the dragon's back. With a final glance toward her new friends, she and Storm moved into the cave and were swallowed by a blaze of light.

Chapter 6

Who are you?" The figure poked Emily with a sharp-pointed spear. Its face was particularly hideous, a viper's open mouth baring long fangs below deadly glowing eyes. A dozen others stood around her, each face more monstrous than the other. Their spears were front and ready.

"My name is Emily. I mean you no harm." She struggled to remain calm.

One of the creatures pointed to her wrist. Her jewel pulsed with reds and blacks. "What is that dark power?" it asked.

"A witch!" came a shout.

"No, I . . ." Emily began.

"Hey, you! Leave her alon-*agggrrrrhhh!*" Ozzie's voice came tumbling down the ravine as the ferret rolled into a heap at Emily's side. *"Doof!"*

He sprang to his feet, boldly pushing the spear away from Emily.

"What is this sorcery?" the creature asked, clearly taken aback by the talking ferret.

"A woodland spirit!" someone shouted.

"*Gah!* I am not a spirit." Ozzie faced the creatures. "Take off that war mask, Crusp. You look like a tree wart!" Ozzie turned to Emily. "Are you all right?"

"I think so," she replied. Emily then noticed that all the short creatures wore wooden masks! Which accounted for the scary faces.

The one Ozzie spoke to stepped back, clearly shaken. "How do you know my name, Spirit?"

"Talk!" Another poked a spear at Ozzie's rump.

"Yeee! Watch it, Tonin! Or I'll tell Aunti Melba to whack your elfish bottom!"

The figures were clearly flabbergasted, talking and muttering to one another.

"And your tag is still stuck on the back!" Ozzie pointed to Crusp's head.

Crusp slipped off his wooden mask. A frightened face with big eyes, bushy eyebrows, and a small nose and mouth greeted them. Masses of curly brown hair flopped over his head. He turned the mask to see his name etched on the back.

The other elves removed their masks as well. They stood about four feet tall, handsome and strong with thickets of long curly hair. Some were clean-shaven, some had neatly trimmed beards and mustaches.

"You know my name. Who are you, Woodland Spirit?" Crusp asked.

"Don't you even recognize your cousin Ozymandius?" Ozzie demanded.

The elves gasped.

"Ozymandius?" another elf stepped forward. "That elf was whisked away by dark forces. He's gone!"

"Well, now I'm back!" Ozzie stomped toward the shaken elves. "And this is my friend Emily. A great mage."

"A mage?!"

"That's right, knothead!" Ozzie said.

"This is nonsense!" Tonin stepped forward. "You . . . you're a . . ."

"Don't say it! The fairimentals transformed me so I could find Emily and her friends."

"Ridiculous! You're all fuzzy!" Crusp exclaimed.

"Ozzie . . ." Emily moaned softly, rubbing at her wrist.

"Have you all gone looney? Elven war masks are for decorating your house. No one *wears* these."

"Goblin riders have come to the Moorgroves. We stand ready to protect our homes!" Tonin declared.

"Ozzie . . ." Emily said again, louder.

"What!" He turned around. "Oo! What is it?" he asked, running to Emily's side.

"That way," she pointed, her wrist ablaze. The pain was worse, which meant someone nearby was also in pain.

The elves looked to the section of woods where she pointed.

"No way!" Crusp stated. "No one goes there. There is darkness and poison."

"Who's sick?" Ozzie leaped to his feet, brazenly facing the elves.

"Brackie and his family," Tonin said, sadly. "They are in isolation."

"Elves are infected?!" Ozzie was jumping up and down. "You bimbots! She can help!"

"She can?" Whispers of suspicion ran through the group.

"Look, you elven wingdip!" Ozzie was out of patience. "Take us to those who are sick! Now!"

Crusp looked to Tonin and the others. "All right," the elf finally said. "But if you use dark magic against us, you will both die."

"Nice talk, Crusp!" Ozzie kicked the elf's leg as they started off down the wide gully. "Coming from an elf who cheated through every game of pushball."

"I did not. You always used a smaller ball — hey!" His eyes flew wide.

"Ohh!" Emily stood but nearly keeled over in pain.

Ozzie was at her side in an instant. "Can you make it?"

Emily's face was covered in sweat. Clearly, she had a fever.

"I'm dizzy . . . feel so weak . . ." she mumbled.

"Hey!" Ozzie called to the elves. "We need some help here!"

The elves gathered around Emily, supporting her. Ozzie had never seen her so weak. "Ready?" he asked, keeping the worry from his voice.

"Yes . . . let's go," she said breathlessly.

"She is very sick for a mage," Tonin commented. "How is she supposed —"

"She'll be okay, just get there — and fast," Ozzie said.

The elves whisked through the thick forests, keeping the drooping girl upright and moving. At the edge of a clearing, they spotted farmland with acres of vegetables and cornlike husks growing in neat rows. The farmhouse lay nestled in a rolling hill beyond. It was a small structure made of wood and stone.

As they crossed, Ozzie saw why the farmland was in isolation. Deep grooves cut through the tall corn, ragged and ugly. Within the grooves, familiar sickly green glowed and pulsed. Black Fire.

Ozzie was heartsick. How could this have happened here?

"The fairimentals have vanished. We are no longer protected," Tonin said, as if reading his mind.

"Ozzie," Emily pointed. Dozens of animals lay in the grass near the side of the house, covered in green glowing wounds.

The group hurried across the field. Opening the wooden front door, Emily found two elves lying listlessly on beds of reed mattresses. Their breathing was shallow, and their skin glowed sickly green.

Emily immediately checked each one. A little elf girl was in her crib. Emily would have to act quickly. "The little one first," she said.

"Stand back! Give her some room!" Ozzie pushed the worried elves back.

Emily pushed her curly hair behind her ears, then raised her wrist. The jewel pulsed erratically, shifting from deep red, to blacks and sparking blues. There was no time to think, no time to worry, only to act.

"Shhh, it's okay little one," she whispered, stroking the baby elf's long hair. Big eyes looked up at her. "What's your name?"

"Vela," the little elf squeaked.

"Don't be afraid, Vela. Just hold my hand."

The small elf hand slipped into Emily's.

The healer closed her eyes — and fell into darkness. Swirling blackness thick as darkest night blanketed her. She fought to stay conscious. The Black Fire had never felt this strong before. It was like a vise locking her in its grip. She had always fought the fire on Earth. Here on Aldenmor, its power was so much stronger, overwheleming.

Emily screamed, making the elves jump.

Ozzie ran to her, leapt, and threw his arm around Emily's neck, as if to hold her in place to keep her from falling. "Hang on, Emily," he whispered.

Emily's jewel pulsed with a surge of rainbow light, slowly at first and then more quickly.

"You can do it," Ozzie hugged her close.

"The ferret is a healer, too?" an elf asked.

"Yes, he helps me." Emily focused harder. Ozzie's words echoed in her clouded vision. She reached for the power as it warped and twisted, like a live snake in her grasp.

Then Emily felt pressure in her hand. The little elf had closed her eyes squeezing Emily's hand as tight as she could.

Emily pushed her will into her jewel. If she faltered now, she would be lost.

Suddenly, the darkness turned lighter. A soft purple haze filtered into her mind, taking form.

The giant fairy creature stood, reaching out great paws, touching Emily with powerful magic.

"Phel!" Emily gasped.

She grabbed for the magic, a lifeline to pull her back from despair.

The rainbow jewel exploded with light, bathing the entire room in cascading pure blue of healing.

Emily grabbed the power, bent it to her will, until she felt little Vela's heartbeat sure and strong. Emily pushed harder. She could feel the fever leaving her body, her vision becoming sharp and clear, focused and strong.

The light faded along with her vision of Phelonius, but Emily no longer felt drained. She was strong, whole again.

She opened her eyes to see Vela sitting up and smiling, no longer covered in sickly green.

Ozzie leaped in front of Vela. "How do you feel?"

"Ooo, a mookrat!" she squealed, squashing the ferret into a big hug. "Can I keep it?"

"Gah!"

A cheer went up from the elves as they surrounded Emily.

"Okay, everyone," Emily smiled, then gently pushed the elves aside to tend to the parents. "Bring the animals to the front of the house, one by one. I'll get to them as soon as I take care of Vela's parents."

The elves made a mad rush to the door, trying to squish through all at once.

"She is a great mage," they rumbled.

"I told you!" Ozzie called out.

"What did you do to Ozzie?" the elves chorused in return.

"Oh, geez," Ozzie slumped forward.

Emily wasted no time. Phel had come to her. Once again, the fairy creature had helped her and in the process, she had discovered something vital. *In healing others, she had healed herself.* Her true path lay in helping — and that was the only true path to herself.

Emily attacked the Black Fire with a vengeance, strengthened with the joy that Phel was alive somewhere on Aldenmor. Finally, all of the sick had been made well.

"We are so grateful," Tonin told Emily when she'd finished her work, "We would be honored if you'd share supper with us."

"We cannot stay. We have to join our friends at Mount Hope," Emily explained.

"We'll take it to go," Ozzie called out, still in the grasp of little Vela's strong hug.

Suddenly, three elves ran through the front door. "Goblin riders!" they exclaimed, breathlessly. "They come!"

"My jewel," Emily said, watching soft rainbow

swirls in the gem. "It's attracted them. We must leave! Can you lead us to Mount Hope?"

"We can take you to the portal at Dream Lake. If it still works, you should arrive nearby." Crusp turned to the elves. "Tonin and I will take them. You take the others to the Far Falls to distract the riders."

"Right!" The elf ran out to tell the others.

"Ozymandius, you have changed," Crusp said, facing the ferret.

"Tell me about it."

"No, I don't mean physically. I mean you have changed. You are . . . a hero."

"Coming from you, Crusp, that's fine praise. Tell her to put some more grain cakes in there, will you, Cousin?"

"Sweetheart, Ozzie has to go now," Emily gently pried the ferret loose from Vela's arms.

"Mooki!" the little elf cried.

"Hush now, darling," her mother said. She handed Emily a bag of goodies. "Come back to us, Healer."

"I'll be back, too." Ozzie gave Vela a kiss. "And next time without fleas!"

Chapter 7

Welcome to the fairy rave."

Kara was awestruck. She couldn't think of a single thing to say! "You're B*Tween!" she finally blurted.

The lead singer stepped forward. Flowing silk scarves swirled around her. She had sparkling azure eyes and cute pointy ears. Dazzling jewels hung from chains around her arms and neck. "I am Sylina, a siren." Her voice was light as air, soft as a cloud.

"I'm Crimson." The red-and-pink-haired percussionist twirled, lightly tapping a rhythm on tiny bells that magically surrounded her like twinkling bubbles. "I'm from the pixie nation." She wore a bright jumpsuit and had bracelets around her ankles and arms. "And I believe this belongs to you," she said finishing the beat on the fairy map before handing it to Kara.

With a spin and bow, the blue-haired instrumentalist introduced herself. "I am Andiluna. A sprightly sprite to my friends. You can call me Andi." She swung her arm striking a thunderous chord from her glowing instrument.

"And you are Kara, the blazing star," the dark-haired siren singer said.

"I love your CD!" was all Kara, completely baffled, could think of to say.

Lyra stood protectively by Kara's side.

"There is no reason to fear us, Lyra." Sylina smiled at the big cat. "Kara is perfectly safe here."

"Fairy raves contain dangerous magic," Lyra spoke.

Crimson's laugh tinkled in the air. "Only some fairies are tricksters, Lyra."

A few nosy hobgoblins landed on Lyra's head, hanging over the cat's face. *"Shooo!"* Lyra shook the pesky creatures away.

"Where are we?" Kara asked, looking around.

"The twilight realm between worlds," Andi told her.

"Huh?"

"Come, walk with us," Sylina led Kara and Lyra away from the curious throngs of fairy creatures. "You are here for answers."

"Everyone, back to the party!" Crimson jumped, sending a row of toadstools spinning around the garden. The crowd began dancing wildly around the thumping drum shapes.

Kara walked among wiggling and dancing

fairies. A little purple spriggle stood, arms crossed, mumbling and scowling at her.

"What's with him?" Kara asked. "I only asked his name."

"It is very rude to ask a fairy his or her name," Sylina said.

"Fairy names are secret. They are only given as a powerful gift," Crimson continued.

"If you trick it into telling you, you capture its magic," Andi explained.

"I'm not up on my fairy etiquette," Kara said. "Sorry, little purple guy."

The spriggle smiled and threw himself onto a crowd of dancing boggles.

Kara had a million questions for Be*Tween. "What are you doing here? Aren't you on tour? What is this place? And how come you're, like, all fairied out?"

Crimson skipped a beat and laughed. "Slow down. First of all, we *are* fairies."

Kara shook her head. "Okay. Go back to where we are."

"You have run the web of magic," Sylina began.

"I did?"

"The web is a bridge between many worlds," the siren singer went on. "But there are different planes of existence known as the astral planes."

"You are in such a place, a twilight realm," Crimson said.

"Fairies spread magic through nature," Sylina explained. "It is elemental, flowing through earth, sky, water, and fire."

"You mean like fairimentals?" Kara asked.

"Fairimentals are guardians of special places of beauty and magic like Aldenmor," Sylina said. "They are the highest power of fairies, existing as pure, flowing energy."

"They are only visible when cloaked in shapes of nature," Andi added.

"Where are they?" Kara asked.

"They have closed themselves off, like a seed, waiting for the rain," Sylina explained.

"So what kind of fairies are you? I mean you're, like, big!" Kara exclaimed.

"We are Be*Tween. We are muses," Sylina continued, "Muses inspire creativity and imagination, powerful forces of magic that connect humans and the fairy realm."

"But you're all over the radio," Kara noted. "And what about your tour?"

"We were called back by a human wizard to protect the fairies of Aldenmor," Crimson said. "You may know of him, Henry Gardener."

"Mr. Gardener? A wizard?" Kara's eyes widened.

"Descended from the great wizards of long ago," Crimson explained.

"Many years ago, humans and magical creatures worked together," Sylina continued slowly. "When the portals between worlds closed, some of the magic remained locked on Earth. Many animals of Earth descend from magical ancestors."

"The same is true for humans as well," Crimson said. "Some humans still carry its seeds. Every few generations the magic becomes strong in them." The trio stared at Kara pointedly.

"But I . . ." Kara's eyes went wide with realization. "You're telling me someone in my, like, great, great, great, past was a magic fairy?" she looked aghast at the spriggles and sproggins dancing around the gardens.

"Not just any fairy, Kara. A fairy queen. Fairy Queen Lucinda, the greatest and most powerful of fairy queens."

Kara rolled her eyes at Lyra. "Fairy Queen, uh-huh."

Everyone knows you're a princess, Lyra quipped.

"Others draw magic from their past, as well," Sylina said seriously, "One has been transformed and now uses magic for evil."

"The Dark Sorceress," Lyra said.

"Yes."

Kara's head was spinning. "This is crazy!"

"The sorceress has released a powerful fairy from the otherworlds. This creature has aligned with the sorceress — in return for the promise of becoming King of the Fairies and ruler of all their magic."

"Powerful fairies can appear in many different guises, flowing from one element to another — shapeshifters," Crimson explained. "This one has potent powers, and it is very dangerous."

Kara's face grew pale. "A shape-shifter. He . . . it came to me," Kara was suddenly frightened of what was being revealed.

Andi told her, "It is called the Skultum. And it is a spellsinging master as well as a powerful fairy."

"You and your friends did well, but the Skultum is not defeated," the raven-haired siren said.

"But I opened those portals!" Kara confessed.

"You did what had to be done," Sylina reassured her, "The fairy map was given to you to open the pathways, to bring magic to Aldenmor."

"There is a darkness spreading across the web, coming from Aldenmor. We called the fairies to this place with our music," Crimson said, "a place of protection, until the web is once again healed. Only the purest of magic can make that happen."

"From only one source," Andi added.

"Avalon," Kara said.

"You must defeat the fairy king and return him to the fairy realms, Kara," Sylina explained, "otherwise he'll spread dark magic through nature."

"How do I do that?" Kara wailed.

"You must get the creature to tell you its true name," Andi said.

"How come you don't you know what its name is?" Kara asked.

"Once we did, but when the Dark Sorceress released the creature from the otherworlds, it took on a new name," Crimson told her.

"Kara, if you get the fairy creature to reveal its true name, you will be granted all of its powers. They will be your own, and the dark fairy will be left powerless."

Kara was beginning to feel this was way over her head.

The band members looked to one another.

"Fairy magic is not always what it appears to be. Sometimes dance, music, riddles, tricks — the most absurd thing can make a fairy forget a secret."

"What, I'm supposed to stand on my head?"

"Very good." Andi clapped. "You're learning."

"But I fell under its power so easily," Kara moaned.

"Kara, no demon can possess you if you maintain the ability to turn and laugh at it," Sylina told her.

82

"Easy for you to say!"

"Not all meanings are meant to be clear at once," Sylina said, "Good luck, Mage, you must join your friends now."

They had arrived back at the raised stone stage. Andiluna picked up a sparkling silver fiddle and began weaving an infectious song. The rave jumped back into full swing as the fairy creatures began leaping and dancing about, hooting and laughing in glorious havoc.

Kara watched Be*Tween rock out. She turned to Lyra.

You have an interesting past, Lyra commented.

"To paraphrase a certain ferret — *Gah!*" Kara said. "Let's go find the others."

Kara opened her backpack and took out the unicorn horn. One hand wrapped around the horn, the other on Lyra's back, she called out, "Take us to our friends at Mount Hope!"

Rainbow beams flowed from the horn's tip, glowing brighter and brighter, bathing them in incandescent light. Then the light began to swirl, faster and faster . . . until a portal yawned open before them.

"Don't give up the spirit of Avalon." She heard Be*Tween call as she and Lyra stepped into the portal and vanished.

Chapter 8

Bright sun broke over the crest of Mount Hope as Kara and Lyra made their way along the dusty trail and up sprawling hillocks at the base of the mountain range. Valleys spread below, and in the far distance the broken landscape of the Shadowlands loomed — a blight upon the land. But here it was relatively green. Tall trees led back to the forests on the western regions. The air was chilly.

"Anything?" Kara asked.

"Over there," Lyra nodded her head toward an outcropping of rocks that covered the openings to a series of caves.

Lyra had picked up a mistwolf call but, it was weak and — tiny. *"It's a mistwolf and it's very angry . . . and scared."*

"Where are the other mistwolves? The pack?"

"I don't know, but there's something else here. I can't make it out."

"We didn't see anything," Kara said.

Suddenly, a growl echoed across the small path. More of a bark, actually.

Lyra nodded toward the rocks.

They advanced slowly. Kara reached inside the backpack for the unicorn jewel. Brandishing it like a weapon, she eyed the surrounding bushes suspiciously. "What is it?" she asked.

"Mistwolf," Lyra replied, cocking her head to listen. She turned and positioned herself in front of Kara.

"Hellooo," Kara called out. "Who's there?"

The growl got louder. One of the bushes began to shake.

"Odd behavior for a mistwolf," Lyra said. *"As if it's protecting the caves."*

Lyra and Kara slowly approached the scary sounds.

Suddenly, a small dog-sized creature leaped from the bush. It was a furry black wolf puppy with white paws and chest.

"Grrrr-uf!" It barked, hackles raised, teeth bared. It lowered its body and leaped forward, trying to attack and with a *yelp* — promptly fell on its nose, stumbling over its too large paws. The pup sprang back to its feet and barked louder.

Lyra regarded the scruffy little pup.

"Kinda small for a mistwolf," Kara said as she watched the fuzzy creature.

"It's a pup," Lyra explained.

"Duh . . . hey little fellow, where's your mommy?" Kara stepped forward.

The pup backed away, snarling.

"I'm going to check out the caves. You keep it occupied."

"How do I —" the little pup lunged and bit Kara's pant leg, shaking his head back and forth.

"Hey, those are Calvins," she complained as she shook him off. She bent down and opened her pack. "How about biting into something you can actually eat?"

She pulled out a granola bar.

The pup carefully sniffed it.

Kara watched Lyra circle around back and enter the caves. "It's okay, see . . . yummmmy," Kara took a small bite. The pup tentatively stepped closer as Kara held out the food. Snapping it away from her fingers, it hungrily began to chew, keeping a wary eye on Kara. It quickly backed away as she tried to pet it.

All at once, Kara felt a sharp pain in her head and deep sadness seep through her. "Lyra, are you all right?" she asked, worried about her friend.

"Yes," came the cat's reply.

Kara saw Lyra emerge from the cave. The pup eyed the cat suspiciously, edging back to give the big animal room.

"*Mistwolves,*" Lyra said

"You found them?"

"*Some.*"

Kara looked into her friend's deep green eyes and knew what Lyra had found in the caves.

"Oh." She looked at the pup sadly, tears welling up in her eyes.

Lyra sharply raised her nose, sniffing the air.

"What is it?"

"*Stormbringer!*"

"And Adriane?"

"*They come.*"

"Thank goodness. What about Emily and Ozzie?"

"*Not yet.*"

Ghostly mist snaked between the trees, and suddenly the great silver mistwolf appeared, hackles raised.

The pup jumped to its feet, stumbling back on its paws.

"Storm!" Kara called out.

The mistwolf stared at Lyra for a second then leaped up the rocky incline and vanished into the caves.

"Hey, Barbie! That you?"

Kara whirled to see Adriane walking around the bend along the rocky path.

"Xena!" Kara cried, running to the dark-haired

girl and catching her friend in a big hug. The girls hugged tightly for a moment, then abruptly stepped back, embarrassed.

"You okay?" Adriane asked.

"Yeah, you?"

Adriane nodded and saw Storm outside the caves. The mistwolf's hackles lay flat, her ears laid back against her head. Then she tilted her head back and let out a mournful howl.

Adriane started to run to her friend, but Kara held her back.

"Oh, no," Adriane cried.

"The mistwolves have been attacked," Storm said.

Twelve had been lost to the enemy.

Adriane squeezed Kara's hand hard, blinking back tears, then walked to look over the bluff at the forests beyond. There were no other mist-wolves in sight — the caves and rocky outcrop-pings appeared to be deserted.

"No sign of the other mistwolves," Lyra said, confirming Adriane's thoughts.

Storm looked down to find the cub standing between her feet.

"Over here!" Adriane was shouting and waving down the ravine.

"I told you we were heading in the right direction!" It was Ozzie.

A moment later Emily's curly hair became visible as she and Ozzie appeared on the path.

"We're here!" Ozzie exclaimed. "Come and hug me!"

"Emily!" Adriane and Kara cried.

Emily raced to embrace her friends.

"I was so worried," Emily said.

"Storm and I were in the Ice Peaks, way up north," Adriane said. "We were helped by friends I met, real merfolk, and they had sea dragons!" Adriane explained breathlessly.

"Wow, that's so cool," Emily laughed.

"Well, I danced with a fairy and met Be*Tween!" Kara said.

"Be*Tween?" Ozzie exclaimed.

"Yeah, cool, huh?"

Emily and Adriane were astounded.

"You found them here — ?" Emily asked, flabbergasted.

"Not exactly here," Kara replied. "They're in an in-between world. Be*Tween are fairy creatures, spellsingers. They're protecting the fairies of Aldenmor."

"Ozzie and I were in the Moorgroves," Emily told her friends. "I'm afraid the Black Fire has spread to other parts of Aldenmor."

Emily heard barking and growling. "Who's

Storm's friend?" she asked. The little wolf was on its back, batting away Storm's playful paws.

"His name is Dreamer," Storm started. *"His parents run with the spirit pack now."*

Emily's face fell. "Hello there, little one." Dreamer let Emily scratch him behind the ears and rub his tummy. "Where are the others, Storm?"

"I don't know. I sense something . . ."

"Well, at least we're all together," Kara said. "I got all kinds of news from Be*Tween."

"They're not shape-shifters are they?" Adriane asked sarcastically.

"No, but they are fairies, real magical stuff."

Adriane eyed the wolf pup, then turned to the others. "Maybe we should get the D'flies to phone Zach. Something's wrong. He should have been here."

"I *am* here!" a familiar voice came from the crest of a hill.

The group turned at the voice. On a high ridge nearby stood a cute boy in a white shirt, beige pants, and sandals.

Adriane gasped. "Zach! Have you been here the whole time?"

"Over here, come quickly!" he called out and disappeared behind the ridge.

"Come on," Adriane took off in a run.

The others followed.

"Something is not right," Storm said.

"There is strong magic somewhere," Lyra said to Storm.

"Yes, mistwolf magic!"

"Hurry!" Adriane called to make sure her friends were right behind her as she ascended the rise.

At the top, she peered down at the boy. He stood in an open field, waving for her to join him. "Here! I have something to show you!" he yelled.

"Zach, what's up?" Adriane asked, worriedly. Heat bit at her wrist. She looked at her stone. The wolf stone pulsed with danger.

The others crested the hill and started down the rise.

Adriane ran toward Zach, but skidded to a stop about ten yards away. Fear tingled up her spine. Her stone was blazing. She looked closely at the strange shimmer cascading around the boy.

Adriane whipped around. "No!" she screamed at her friends. "Go back!"

"Adriane," Storm called, leaping down the hill, teeth bared.

The hair along Lyra's back rose, and a low growl rumbled in her throat.

Dark clouds of mist seemed to fill the valley as if out of thin air.

The mist fell away, and the valley was completely full. Huge, horrid nightmares snorted fire, training red eyes on the trapped group. Upon their backs sat armored goblins, fierce and deadly. And behind them stood short, black as ink, faceless imps, at least one hundred strong.

Adriane watched in horror as Zach walked right up to the goblin leader atop the biggest and most frightening of the nightmares. The boy's eyes narrowed to evil yellow slits, then glowed blood red. His body seemed to melt as it changed to a shadowy lizard form. It continued past the riders, vanishing behind the attackers.

"Zach, no," Adriane said, feeling her tears threaten to fall.

"How is that possible?" Ozzie asked. "They appeared out of nowhere — like the mistwolves."

"They are using the magic of the mistwolves," Storm told them. *"The mistwolves are lost."*

"Form a circle!" Adriane screamed.

Trying to stop shaking, Emily, Adriane, and Kara stood back to back, to face the impossible enemy.

Storm, Lyra, and Ozzie surrounded the trio, ready to sacrifice themselves to protect their friends. Dreamer stood between Storm's front feet, growling and barking.

"Kara, stand between us," Adriane ordered, moving Kara. "Focus, Kara! We hit the lead riders first!"

The imps stood their ground as the goblin riders approached.

"There's too many!" Kara screamed.

"Kara, the horn!" Emily reminded her, urgently.

"Ooo!" Kara reached into her pack and removed the unicorn horn. It sparkled like a diamond in the sun.

The lead goblin raised a clawed fist and pulled his fierce steed to a halt. "You will come with us either way," it hissed.

"Leave us alone!" Adriane shouted out. "Or you'll regret it!"

The goblin's apelike head grinned. Its pointed teeth made it look like a deranged Halloween pumpkin.

"The imps!" Storm shouted.

Electrical sparks danced in the air as a swarm of imps came at the group from all sides. Flashing blue crackled along wide nets strung between them.

They were hopelessly outnumbered.

"Don't be afraid," Ozzie said to his friends.

"Emily," Kara said, terrified as she pushed the horn at the red-haired girl.

"Hold it up, Kara." Emily said.

Trembling, Kara held the unicorn horn as high as she could in the air.

"Lorelei!" The three girls called to the magic of the unicorn. "Protect us!"

The sky exploded with fire.

The girls shielded their faces from the intense heat as flames flew overhead.

But it was not the fire born of magic jewels.

It was the fire of a tremendous winged creature, a flying monster.

The huge beast swooped in, its massive wings cutting through the smoke and flames, making it hard to see exactly what it was.

"Oh, no!" Emily exclaimed.

"The manticore!" Kara screamed.

There was nowhere to go. The magic of the horn had failed them. They were completely surrounded.

Chapter 9

Pandemonium erupted in the field. Blue lightning flashed as plumes of smoke sent shadowy imps scurrying everywhere. Screams, yells, snorts, and roars added to the chaos.

"Stay together!" Adriane commanded, swinging her arm, tearing swatches of bright gold light through the smoke and haze.

The girls remained in position, jewels glowing and ready.

"Hey! They're running away!" Kara pointed.

The imps sparked with blue electricity as they moved away from the group, their nets disintegrated.

Ozzie jumped up and down shaking his fist, "And don't come back — uh-oh!"

But the imps had only retreated behind the leading edge of goblin riders. Nightmares reared, snorting flames, adding to the thick smoke flowing across the field. The riders held bright red staffs high, ready to release dark lightning as they bore down on the group, coming in fast.

Kara held up the unicorn horn as Emily and Adriane reached to touch Kara's hands. Gold and blue flew from the rainbow jewel and the wolf stone, swirling up Kara's arms and into the horn.

Adriane pulled the unicorn horn, pointing it to the ground in front of the incoming riders. Magic exploded forth. Four nightmares were blown to the sides, their riders flying as grass and dirt rained everywhere. Six more nightmares jumped the open fissure, firing lightning from their staffs.

Adriane and Storm leaped into the fire's path, spinning a shield of sparkling gold around themselves. Mistwolf and girl worked like a fine-tuned machine, whirling and turning to block every bolt, sending them exploding harmlessly into the air.

But the nightmares were strong and fast, barreling past Adriane straight toward Emily and Kara. Lyra pushed the girls behind her, teeth bared, wings unfurled, ready to absorb the crushing impact.

With a roar, a huge red tail swept through the haze, knocking the goblins off their mounts. The mutant horses ran, missing the group by yards. Emily and Kara felt fire breath heat as they passed.

The creature stood in front of the girls roaring defiantly at the goblins and imps. The attacking hoard was backing away over the far ridge, leaving the group, for now.

"That's not the manticore!" Ozzie exclaimed.

"What is it?" Emily asked, trembling.

The fierce creature turned a horselike head on its long sinewy neck. It was as big as a bus with a long tail covered in glimmering red scales. Large reptilian eyes narrowed dangerously as it snorted. With a rush, it stomped toward them on massive hind legs.

Something opened inside Adriane's mind. Something familiar, strong, and right — feelings of love rushed through her mind and body, it was like . . . coming home.

"That's a dragon!" Ozzie screamed.

Kara grabbed for Emily's and Adriane's hands.

"No, wait!" Adriane cried.

The dragon lumbered toward them, practically stumbling on its enormous feet. When it was only a few feet away, it stopped, folding its shimmering, iridescent wings. Smoke drifted from its nostrils as it leaned forward, opened its huge mouth —

"Momma!"

— and licked Adriane so hard, she was lifted several feet into the air.

"Drake?" Adriane said as she landed on the ground. "It *is* you!" She threw her arms around

Drake's neck, hugging the dragon as tight as she could. Then she stepped back to look him in the eye. "Wow. You've really grown!"

The dragon was happily shuffling back and forth from foot to foot, tongue lolling out. *"Momma! Momma!"*

THUD!

The ground shook as Drake rolled over onto his back, legs and arms akimbo, waiting for Adriane to scratch his belly.

"Tickle!"

Adriane giggled, reaching over to rub the great creature's amazingly soft belly. "I missed you so much!"

The group watched, mouths opened in stunned silence.

"Well, now I've seen everything!" Ozzie stomped over to inspect the dragon.

Emily smiled. "It's Adriane's baby dragon."

"Some baby," Kara muttered as she nervously scanned the skies. For all she knew, full-sized dragons traveled in packs like the pesky dragonflies. She could *not* handle another fan club — especially not one with members as big as Drake.

"Don't worry," Lyra told her, reading her mind. *"Dragons are one of a kind. The red dragons hatch only once every thousand years."* She eyed Adriane and Drake. *"He's imprinted on Adriane,"* she added.

"Everybody, this is Drake," Adriane said, introducing the dragon to her friends.

"Hello!" Drake snorted, sitting up. The dragon's lips parted, revealing rows and rows of razor-sharp teeth. Kara hoped it was a smile.

"Dragons grow very quickly," Storm explained.

"You can say that again," Kara replied.

Adriane first met Drake when he was still inside his egg. When she left Aldenmor, he'd barely hatched. She knew that dragon magic was incredibly powerful, but she never expected her friend to grow so fast.

"Such a sweet boy," Adriane cooed, playfully scratching Drake under his chin. The dragon laughed, shooting sparks out his nostrils. A small fireball shot out of his mouth.

Emily, Kara, and the others leaped back.

"Ahh!!" Ozzie shouted. "Try and keep it on low flame!"

"Sorry," Drake said, hanging his head over Adriane's.

"Drake, where's Zach?" Adriane suddenly realized Drake had flown in by himself. She tried to keep the worry out of her voice.

"He went after Moonshadow and the mistwolves," Drake replied. He sounded worried himself. *"Zach told me to stay outside so the witch would not capture me."*

"Wait, if that wasn't Zach, then who — oh." Kara flashed on what Be*Tween had told her of the dark fairy.

"That wasn't Zach, and I'll give you two guesses who it really was," Adriane said grimly.

"That means Zach is captured, in a spell somewhere," Emily said.

"I have not heard from Zach at all," Drake admitted. *"Then I heard you in my mind and came here."*

"The Dark Sorceress has the mistwolves," Storm said. *"That is the only way she could be using their magic."*

"But how is that possible, Storm?" Adriane asked.

"I do not know. It takes very strong magic to capture or kill a mistwolf," Storm said.

Drake nodded, shuffling on his huge feet again. *"Have not heard from Zach!"*

"If she has Moonshadow," Adriane figured, "then she has his fairy map. And she must be using it to open the portals."

"The map was given to Moonshadow," Storm insisted. *"Fairy magic only works for those it is given. He would guard that map with his life."*

"Perhaps he doesn't have the strength to prevent it," Lyra said quietly.

There was a long moment of silence as the

group considered this sobering thought — and another that nobody wanted to say aloud: Maybe Moonshadow *had* defended the map with his life.

"What else did Be*Tween tell you, Kara?" Emily asked.

"Um, long story," Kara said. "But they're in an in-between world. They told me the shape-shifter is really an evil fairy and it's going to spread magic when it comes."

"You mean like Phel spreading magic seeds?" Emily asked.

"That's what fairies do," Ozzie said. "They spread magic through nature."

"An evil fairy would use the magic to poison nature," Emily reasoned.

"Wait a minute," Adriane said. "The merfolk told me they were waiting for the magic rain."

"They didn't know whether it would be light or dark rain," Storm added. *"Good or bad magic."*

"Maybe the sorceress has opened portals, but there's no more magic," Emily suggested.

"No, no . . ." Ozzie was pacing back and forth, thinking.

"Or she hasn't found what she needs yet," Kara added.

"No, no . . ." Ozzie came to a stop. "The portals opened in a sequence. I think she opened the pipeline but can't start the magic flow."

"So she's found what she wants," Emily said, hoping she was wrong.

"Avalon," Ozzie said.

"It's possible."

Adriane sighed. "Anything is possible."

The three girls looked at one another but didn't speak. They didn't have to: They were all thinking the same thing. Anything was possible, but their task here on Aldenmor felt totally impossible. And they still didn't have any real answers. Just possibilities.

"One thing is for sure," Adriane finally said. "We have to go after Zach and the mistwolves."

"Well, we can't sit around here," Ozzie agreed. "Those goblins will be back any second. Probably with some orcs or worse!"

"We can't just waltz into the dark circle, either," Kara reminded them.

"She already knows we're here," Storm said.

"Then why didn't she attack us?" Emily asked. "We could have walked into a trap at the dark circle."

"Because."

They all looked at the ferret.

"She's afraid," Ozzie said.

"Of us?"

"Of course," Ozzie started shuffling back and forth. "Whatever she's doing, she doesn't want us anywhere near her place. She tried to take us out, all together, right here."

"So if we can get into the lair before those riders and imps regroup, maybe we have a chance!" Adriane hit her palm with a fist.

"Okay, but that's gotta be, like, miles from here," Kara looked toward the desolate plains beyond the open valleys. "How are we going to get there before the monsters attack us again?"

Adriane smiled and patted the dragon's neck. "Welcome to Air Drake."

"Oy, why did I think you were going to say that?" Ozzie replied.

Chapter 10

They slid off Drake's back as the dragon landed smoothly behind a large dune overlooking the Shadowlands. Lyra set down alongside, her magic wings folding and disappearing with a soft glow.

"This is it?" Kara asked incredulously.

It was hard to believe that this burned-out desert had once been lush, vibrant, and full of life. It was even harder to believe that the small band of travelers had any hope of restoring it.

Three girls, cat, mistwolves, ferret, and dragon peered over the gray ridge. Steam hissed across the barren landscape before them. Several rounded structures rose from the sandlike smokestacks. An open stone courtyard led to a pair of black doors leaning into the first tower.

"There's more," Lyra growled. *"Below."*

The Dark Sorceress's lair lay largely hidden underground. Adriane and Lyra were well aware of the vast caverns, catacombs, and labyrinth of mazes that wormed under the surface.

Adriane felt her stomach tighten, and a trickle of sweat trailed down her neck. She was back to a place out of her worst nightmares, a place she thought she'd never return to. And yet, here she was. The last time she had barely escaped, and that was with the help of the entire pack. Where was the pack now?

Storm sensed her friend's dread. *"Stay focused, warrior. Turn fear to strength. Use it."*

"What's that, Storm? Those weren't here before." Adriane pointed to several triangular crystals that pierced the ground in the center of the towers.

"Zach told us she was building those," Emily reminded them.

"That's where she's going to store the magic," Ozzie said.

The squirming wolf pup in Emily's arms sniffed the air and barked.

"Shhh. We have to be very quiet," Emily said, putting the pup on the ground.

"Good point, Dreamer," Kara said. "How do we get past those?" Kara's gaze was on the entrance to the lair.

Tall serpentine guards walked in groups out of

the doors, each holding long staffs that reflected sun in sparks of light. From around the base of the distant funnel, goblin riders rode patrol. Their nightmare beasts snorted, the goblins on their backs scowled into the distance.

"Won't be long before they sense us here," Lyra said.

Kara sucked in her breath. "Okay, so, what's the plan?"

"We go in under Mistwolf cover, then find Zach and the mistwolves," Adriane said.

"Right," Kara nodded. "So we don't have a plan."

"We stay on course, moving forward," Adriane responded.

"Cannot hear Zach!" Drake's voice echoed loudly in everyone's head.

Adriane looked into the dragon's deep crystalline eyes. They swirled in distressful shades of red and orange. "We need you to help us, Drake."

The dragon's eyes lit up with greens and blues. *"Yes, I help Zach!"*

"Yes. But you have to stay out here."

Drake's head drooped in disappointment, steam leaking from his nostrils. *"I help!"*

"You have a very important job," Adriane explained carefully. "When I say so, you have to create a diversion."

The dragon looked confused.

"Make lots of loud noise, swoop up and down, and keep the guards distracted."

"I can do that."

"Good dragon," Adriane said. "Wait for my call. And if any of the others that attacked us show up, let me know right away."

"Okay," Drake snorted.

Adriane reached up and hugged the dragon's neck, giving him a kiss on his wide nose. "We'll find Zach."

"What about Dreamer?" Kara asked.

The little mistwolf stood shyly next to Storm.

Adriane bent low to face the little guy. "You're a brave boy, aren't you, Dreamer?"

The mistwolf snarled and barked, showing Adriane his fiercest face.

Adriane smiled.

The dark-haired warrior stood and faced the others. "All right. We'll take him with us."

Adriane extended her arm. Emily put her hand on top of Adriane's. Kara's hand covered theirs. Ozzie, Storm, and Lyra stood close by.

The three girls looked into one another's eyes. There was only one thing to say.

"Let's do it!" Adriane said firmly.

Stormbringer shimmered under the hazy bright sun. A second later, her body disappeared — transforming into a thick white fog. Dreamer watched with interest as the silky mist thinned and slowly settled over the group.

From the desert floor, the dark riders and guards fanned out, carefully watching the skies. They didn't notice the swirling haze as it moved toward the double doors.

The tight group slipped quickly behind the doors, and instantly were swallowed in darkness.

"Which way, Storm?" Adriane whispered.

"Down."

❧ ❧ ❧

Cloudy images surfaced in the crystal-pure water. The Dark Sorceress bent over her seeing pool, stirring it with a single sharp claw. She waited for the pictures to clear.

A slow snarl curled the corner of her thin lips as she narrowed her animal eyes. A sparkling bubble burst in the pool. When it cleared, it revealed a room filled with three enormous crystals. The picture faded as another bubble rose to the surface and a new image floated before her — a small cloud drifting down a corridor toward the vast chamber of crystals.

"You see. It is like I told you!" She spoke to the tall, dark shape standing near her. Her claw retracted into a slender finger. "They have come."

The dark fairy glowered, as its body shimmered and flowed. It was called the Skultum, a being made of pure transcendence and energy. "These humans are incorrigible!" the thing hissed.

"You have no idea," the witch said in a velvety voice.

"The sequence of portals is opened, just as I said it would be," the Skultum groveled, trying to regain favor.

The Dark Sorceress swung at the hideous creature, her long robes whispering to the ground like a silent shroud. "You are a powerful fairy creature, are you not?"

"Yes, my mistress."

Waves of fear fouled the sorceress's sharp senses. She hated this mutant creature, but she had called it, releasing it from the forbidden otherworlds. At least it knew its place. And it still had a job to do. Complete and utter subservience was essential.

"Yet you could not unlock the map yourself. And worse, you let it fall back into the hands of these . . . these mages!"

"Mages!" The Skultum laughed, a hideous cackle. "They are merely girls!"

"You know nothing!" She snarled, spitting viciously, making the Skultum back up in alarm.

"These *girls* have power! These *girls* channel the fairimentals themselves!" The sorceress's voice rose in voracity. "These GIRLS channel magic through animals! The very lifeblood of Aldenmor channels through their jewels! So do not speak to me of what they can or cannot do!" The witch shuddered, then calmed.

The dark fairy stood silent, waiting.

"When the magic collects in the crystals, I trust you will do what you have agreed to."

The Skultum stepped into the light of the seeing pool. Reflections rippled over its distorted face, melting between flesh and bone. "I will drive the dark magic into the fabric of Aldenmor itself, through fairy magic, and it will be yours to command, my mistress."

"Then you shall have the fairy realms to do with as you wish."

The Skultum's mouth dissolved into a deathlike grin.

"But, my dear fairy king . . . you as yet do not possess both maps." The half-woman, half-animal smoothed back her silver blond hair to gaze at the fairy map floating above a pedestal just near the pool — the map she had taken from the fallen mistwolf. The map was fairy magic and such, only those it was intended for could use it. Combined with the other map, all secrets would unlock.

She needed the second map — *and* the blazing star to open them.

Both were already on their way.

The sorceress extended a claw from her fingertip and dipped her hand back into the pool, swirling the tainted liquid. The images faded as the Skultum began to weave its magic.

The creature shimmered and glowed, arms moving in hypnotic patterns, conjuring, casting. Then, arching its back, the Skultum began to chant a series of guttural, unintelligible words. They jumbled together, flowing, echoing in the chamber, a raw combination of animal grunts and melody. The power grew, palpable and electrical in the air. Then, with a wave of its serpentine claws, the Skultum unleashed the powerful spellsong of binding, sending it to the one it knew would have to answer.

❦ ❦ ❦

The group silently made its way crisscrossing through dank, dark tunnels. Lights flashed in the distance. They neared a wide connecting corridor where the tunnel split into three adjoining passageways. At the end of one, red flames pulsed with heat, as shadow shapes scurried to and fro.

"The mistwolves are there," Storm's voice spoke through the mist.

"What about Zach?" Emily asked.

Adriane concentrated on her wolf stone, trying to keep her magic contained yet strong enough to get a reading from the dragon stone that Zach possessed. She got nothing.

"Let's find the mistwolves first, then," Ozzie suggested.

They silently moved up the right corridor, heading into the heat that poured through the tunnel.

They came to a wide doorway cut out of the rock itself. Beyond lay an immense cavern. Staying close to the shadowy walls, they snuck inside. Blinding light shone from three gigantic crystals towering in the center of the enormous chamber.

"Incredible!" Emily said in shock, craning her neck to see the tops of the crystals cut off by the ceiling. The rest of the crystals were on the surface.

"Oh, my!" Ozzie exclaimed, wide-eyed.

The girls had learned how powerful their jewels could be. But here, before them, these gigantic crystals dwarfed anything they could have possibly imagined. What power these giant jewels must have!

The magic these crystals could hold was beyond comprehension — as was the destruction they'd caused. Here was the *source* of the black fire, poisonous residue released from the sorceress's attempts to construct these monolithic giants.

Turn back, the voice of a mistwolf whispered in Adriane's head.

"Storm?" Adriane strained to see in the chamber, but the blanket that was Storm still covered the group.

Save yourselves, Little Wolf Daughter, the voice hissed. *Run!*

The voice was familiar — but it wasn't Storm.

"Silver Eyes!" Adriane cried.

The veil of mist swept from the group as Storm took shape, leaping into the chamber.

"What is that?" Ozzie asked.

With the veil removed, they could see the crystals were filled with a churning, roiling mist.

"Mistwolves," Storm snarled, making her way behind the first towering crystal. *"They're trapped inside."*

That would explain how the sorceress held them. Only cages of glass or crystal could contain mistwolves, prevent them escaping into mist.

"Storm, wait!" Adriane tried to stay calm. Shadows were moving toward them from the far side of the chamber.

"What's happening to them?" Ozzie asked, horrified.

"Their magic is being drained." Storm said from across the chamber. *"They cannot exist in mist form for much longer, or they will die."*

Dreamer barked and jumped to the shallow cavern floor, racing after Storm.

"How do we get them out?" Ozzie was frantically jumping up and down.

"Kara, hold up the horn!" Adriane pulled back her sleeve to release her wolf stone. The time for stealth was over. Things were getting out of control — and fast.

"Kara?" Emily asked, looking around, voice tight, like it was hard to breathe.

"She was right here a second ago!" Ozzie ran to look down the corridor. It was empty.

"Lyra, what happened?" Adriane asked.

Lyra paced, growling low in her throat. The fur on the back of her neck stood up. *I don't know. Something blocks my senses. I can't feel Kara!*

"Kara?" Adriane called, panic rising, threatening to topple her resolve.

"Kara!" Emily called for the third time. She was practically shouting, in spite of the danger.

There was no reply. Kara was gone.

The ground beneath their feet fell away, sending them sliding into darkness.

Chapter 11

S torm?" Adriane called out. "Can you hear me?"

Jewel light flashed erratically across the dark space.

"Are you . . . all right?" Storm's reply was broken, strained in static.

"Yeah, what's happening?"

"I am linked . . . mistwol — Holding them . . . from fading."

Adriane wanted desperately to be with her friend to help.

"Is everyone all right?" Emily used her light to search the room.

Lyra's magic wings unfurled as the big cat peered up through the open chute that had deposited them. She leaned back, ready to leap.

"No, Lyra. We have to stick together!" Adriane brushed the cat's raised hackles.

"Kara's up there, alone!" the cat hissed.

"Can you sense anything, Lyra?" Emily asked.

The cat closed her eyes, then shook her head. *"She is under a spell. I cannot reach her."*

Emily stroked Lyra's head and sent as much calm as she could into the cat's worried green eyes. "We'll find her. Okay?"

Gahfphooot!

"Ozzie? Where's Ozzie?" Emily beamed light across the barren room.

The ferret was stuck headfirst in a mound of dirt.

Adriane and Emily ran across the room and pulled him out by his feet.

"Spoof!"

"Are you all right?"

"How could I be so stupid!" Ozzie kicked the pile of dirt, sending dust flying. Particles hung in the air caught in beams of gold and blue.

"It's not your fault, Ozzie," Emily consoled him, arms around her chest. It was creepy, dank, and cold in there.

"We know she's susceptible to spellsinging!" Ozzie brushed dirt from his head and stomped around. "Now she's under another spell."

"You think the shape-shifter is here?" Emily whispered.

"I would bet on it! And we brought Kara right into its clutches." Ozzie looked around. "Where are we?"

"The dungeons," Adriane pushed away the dirt that had broken Ozzie's fall. "Help me here."

Emily and Lyra, working with Adriane, quickly swept away the dirt. A door was hidden behind it.

"I think you found the way out, Ozzie," Emily observed.

"Always had a nose for direction."

"Stand back!" Adriane shouted, raising her arm. The wolf stone pulsed with power. She swung once and a wave of golden power smashed into the door. With a loud *Poof!* the door flew open into a wide corridor.

The four made a run for it. Soft lights cast pale illumination from crystals imbedded in the walls. Long shadows seemed to slip and curl as if the tunnels were alive.

Emily noticed Lyra gazing up and down the darkened corridor, her green-gold eyes narrowed slightly. Not that long ago, the cat had been held prisoner here along with other magical animals. Lyra, horribly wounded, had escaped. Emily shuddered, thinking of how hard it must be for the cat to return to this terrible place.

"I sense something," Lyra said as she sniffed the air in the narrow hall. The fur on her neck was just beginning to relax. *"Someone's alive. Human."*

Adriane's eyes lit up. "Where?"

"This way," Lyra said, taking off down the darkened passageway.

The group followed, making their way into the catacombs that held the prison cells. The jagged hallway was lined with heavy doors, and the group split up to listen at each one.

Adriane took the doors at the very end. Each time she raised her wolf stone to sense beyond the cold metal and wood, she tried to push the apprehension and fear from her mind. The golden glow that emanated from her stone seemed tiny in the huge darkness of the catacombs. Somehow she knew that Storm was getting weaker.

Storm! Hang on, Adriane sent a message to her friend.

"Over here!" Emily called out, summoning everyone to the door she was standing at.

This time Adriane whipped a ring of gold and clasped the metal bars in the small window. She pulled hard. The others helped raise as much power from the wolf stone as they could. With a creak, the door opened into darkness.

They practically stumbled over the still figure on the floor.

"Zach!" Adriane cried, falling to her knees and searching the boy's ashen face for a sign of life. She saw the red dragon stone he wore on his wrist softly blink.

Emily was beside her in an instant, rainbow jewel pulsing strong. "He's in a trance, the Skultum's spell."

Lyra growled low nearby.

The healer wasted no time. She held out her jewel, sending out a beam of healing blue light.

There was no response. Emily gazed down at Zach's barely moving chest. The boy was in bad shape. He seemed too far away to be reached.

"He's been under awhile! Help me," Emily called out. Ozzie, Lyra, and Adriane pressed around her, concentrating on sending their own energy to break the spell. Emily, supported by her friends, focused her will. Her jewel flashed bright and fast and Emily felt a flutter of activity. The dragon stone flashed. Zach's heartbeat was strengthening, his breathing deepening.

Zach opened his eyes and blinked. "Adriane, you're in my dreams."

Adriane hugged the boy, her heart full of joy. "No dream, Zach."

They helped him sit up.

"What are you doing here?" he said, groggily.

"Rescuing you," Adriane said.

"Guess we're even," Zach smiled weakly.

"ZACH!"

"Agghh!" Zach covered his ears as the voice of Drake exploded in his head.

"Ooo, sorry, are you all right?"

"I *was* . . . yeah, okay."

Adriane told me to wait outside and make lots of noise when she tells me. I help!

"Okay, stay there," Zach instructed the dragon.

"How long have you been here?" Emily asked, rubbing Zach's arms to help circulation.

"I don't know," he said. "Last thing I remember, I had snuck into the lair, trying to contact the mistwolves — then I fell out."

"Zach, we found the crystals you told us about," Adriane told him.

"Where are the mistwolves?" Zach asked, his face growing grim.

"Trapped inside them," Emily finished.

"We have to get them out!" He pushed himself up — then slid back down, "Ow, my legs are numb."

"Easy, you have to stay still for a while," Emily said.

A sleek feline shape darted noiselessly through the door. *"I can't find a clear way out. I keep going in circles."*

"I got out last time," Adriane said.

"The sorceress *let* you get out to try and lure in the mistwolves," Ozzie reminded her.

"Yeah, you're right," Adriane remembered.

Zach wiped matted blond hair from his forehead. "This time she got them."

"And Kara, too," Emily added.

"Kara?" Zach surveyed the rescue party realizing they were one member short.

"She's under a spellsinging spell," Ozzie informed him.

"That's fairy magic!" Zach exclaimed.

"The sorceress is working with a fairy creature," Adriane said. "A shape-shifter."

Zach sighed. "Fairy magic. That's what called the mistwolves and trapped them in the crystals."

"But why?" Emily asked.

"Mistwolf magic, of course," Ozzie said. "Magic attracts magic. She's using the mistwolves to draw magic into the crystals, where she can use it."

"That's why she's been hunting magical animals," Adriane said.

"No doubt she's gotten Moonshadow's fairy map," Zach said soberly. "Luckily, the fairimentals safeguarded the magic of the maps."

"What do you mean?" Emily asked.

"She may have opened portals," Zach explained. "But in order to find the source of the magic, she would need *two* fairy maps."

Everyone was startled — and concerned.

"What?" Zach asked.

"Kara has the second map," Adriane told him.

Zach struggled to get up again. "We have to get the mistwolves out. They can't survive in there."

"Storm is keeping them strong," Adriane said, her voice strained and cracking.

"She's only one wolf, she can't hold on to them for long!" Zach saw Adriane's face go white — he stopped talking.

The warrior got up and paced. She lifted her stone, sending a silent message to Storm. *"Storm, we found Zach,"* she told her pack mate. *"But Kara is missing. How are you doing?"*

"I am with you," came Storm's staticky reply.

"She's okay," Adriane could not hide the worry plainly visible on her face.

Lyra yowled, trying to reach Kara but to no avail.

"Some mages we turned out to be!" Adriane slumped next to Zach, head in her hands. What were they going to do? They had found Zach and he was okay. But the situation had gone from bad to horrible. Soon it would be hopeless.

❧   ❧   ❧

The door to the throne room opened, and Kara stepped inside. Caught in the powerful spellsong, she felt like some sort of marionette, and she could not resist its pull.

"Come in, child." The Dark Sorceress was atop her high stone thrown. She was tall and striking. Long silver-blond hair slashed with white lightning streaks fell over her shoulders and down her back.

Her robe glided silently over the stone floor as the sorceress stood and came to Kara.

Then Kara saw the eyes. She had seen them before, the cold eyes of a beast. Vertical slits opened, pinning Kara in their icy stare.

Kara shivered, even though she didn't feel cold. She opened her mouth to speak, but nothing came out.

The witch moved long fingers.

"— me go!" Kara finished.

"Tsk, tsk. We have so much to catch up on, my dear," Her eyes bore into Kara's. "And you *must* tell me everything."

Kara watched, a prisoner inside her own head, her own body. "Yes."

"Perfection," the witch coldly inspected Kara. "With proper guidance, your power will be grand. You like using the magic, don't you?"

"Yes," Kara said honestly. She couldn't stop the words, as if they were being drawn out of her.

"I know you do. You're going to show me what you can do," the witch spoke firmly.

"Yes,"

"Good." The Dark Sorceress smiled, fangs gleaming.

Kara would have run screaming out of the room if she could've moved her feet.

"Well, come on, show me what you have brought," the witch commanded.

Kara struggled. A part of her knew she shouldn't — she couldn't resist. She reached into her backpack and felt cold fire. Power raced up and down her arm like a thousand pinpricks. With her eyes locked onto the sorceress, Kara pointed the unicorn horn at the witch. It blazed with light. But Kara could not release its magic.

The witch's animal eyes glowed with delight. The horn flew from Kara into her evil grasp. The light faded, cracks spiraled up and down. With a twist of her wrist, the horn splintered to dust, cascading to the floor like snow.

Kara watched helplessly.

"You know what I want!" she demanded.

"No!" Kara screamed silently. She willed her body to flee, then watched, horrified, as her sparkling fairy map floated gently into the air. At that moment, another map, almost identical, lifted from a pedestal nearby and drifted, drawn by its twin's magic.

"You realize only powerful fairy magic can use the maps," the witch said cooly.

"Yes, Be*Tween told me." What was she saying? But she couldn't help herself.

"Be*Tween? Ah, fairy spellsingers, of course."

The witch smiled, tapping her chin with a long claw. "Fairies are tricksters. They are users, like the fairimentals. They will use anything or anyone to get what they want."

Kara stood motionless as the Dark Sorceress circled her like a viper.

"They told you that you have fairy blood?"

"Yes, from Queen Lucinda," Kara answered.

"But they didn't tell you the rest." The witch stopped to watch Kara's confused expression.

She stared into Kara's eyes. "There is a reason you and I are alike, child. Lucinda was my sister."

Kara gasped. It can't be! But deep inside, she'd known the terrible truth, there was a bond between her and the sorceress. She'd felt it when they'd first met. The sorceress had even told her as much — but Kara refused to believe it.

"Open yourself to the truth." The witch's words bore into Kara like poison. "Embrace the magic that lies inside of you. And let it out!"

Music filled Kara's head, words so soothing and luxurious. For the first time, she noticed a tall, dark shape standing in the shadows, green scales running along sinewy arms raised in the dim lights.

Kara's arms waved in front of her in patterns she didn't recognize. She was confused at first, but it soon became clear that *she* was beckoning the fairy maps. They responded immediately. Floating side by side, pulsing and growing larger, they got closer.

Then, with a spark, the two maps converged and drifted over Kara. Star lines charged with electric energy surrounded her. Tiny points of light twinkled like diamonds.

Kara couldn't think. The maps were so incredibly beautiful.

"Use the fairy map," the firemental had told her. Is this what she was supposed to do?

"If you have fairy magic, why don't *you* use them?" Kara managed to get out.

The witch turned away, but not before Kara saw a hint of — sadness?

"I have traveled beyond what I once was," the Dark Sorceress said, then faced Kara again, eyes aflame. "Now, show me where the magic lies!"

Points of light began to flash in sequence, the strands of the web glowed.

Kara fought to clear her mind and regain control. But surrounded in the pathways of magic and under the spellsong, she could not stop what had begun. She felt helpless and for the first time . . . totally alone.

Chapter 12

T his place is nothing but a maze!" Zach complained, frustrated.

The group had struggled along, using all their senses and jewels combined to find the right way through the catacombs. Exhausted, they had arrived at another wide intersection with connecting tunnels.

"How are you doing?" Adriane asked Zach.

"Fine." He slumped against the wall. He was still weak from the spell.

"I have navigated these passageways before," Lyra shook her head. *"But the path lies hidden from me."*

There was a moment of depressed silence.

"Let's rest here for a few minutes," Emily suggested.

Adriane slid down next to Zach. Emily and Ozzie joined them, huddled close together. Nobody spoke. The only sound was the *pad, pad, pad* of Lyra's paws on the stone floor as she paced, examining each joining tunnel for the correct way back to the surface.

Adriane sighed. Hopelessness washed over her, making her feel even more tired than she was.

"You know, you're so lucky," Zach said to Adriane, then looked to the others. "All of you."

"Lucky?" Adriane echoed. "What do you mean?"

"I grew up alone. I never knew what it's like to have friends. Except for Windy, of course, and now Drake."

Everyone turned to Zach.

"Then I met you." He looked at Adriane, who blushed. "You have the best friends in the world."

"It wasn't always that way," Emily said, remembering.

"Yeah, when we first met Kara, we couldn't stand her," Adriane smiled.

"Really?"

"Oh, yeah, she was the self-appointed miss perfect Barbie princess of popularity," Adriane said.

"So what happened?" Zach asked, clearly interested.

Emily snorted. For a second, Adriane thought the redheaded girl was crying. But when Emily snorted again, it was clear that she was laughing.

"She's just so . . . so likable," Emily explained. "She's smart, funny, confident —"

"Pink," Adriane added, smiling.

"Remem —" Emily laughed again. "Remember when Kara had to talk to the whole school and the dragonflies stole her hat?"

Adriane nodded. Who could forget?

"That look on her face when her hat came off and her hair came tumbling out — rainbow-colored!" Tears were streaming down Emily's face. She could not stop cracking up.

Adriane laughed. "Yeah, she freaked."

"How'd that happen?" Zach asked.

Adriane recounted the story for Zach of Kara's magical bad-hair day. "Emily totally saved her," she explained. "She said that Kara had dyed her hair to symbolize the true meaning of Ravenswood, a tapestry of friends." Adriane was cracking up now, too.

"I think the best part of friends is having those memories you share, moments that make you feel so good inside." He smiled. "I'll never forget the feeling I got flying with Windy. Always makes me smile."

"I don't see my friends from Colorado anymore," Emily said. "But I still remember hot summer days and the old rope swing that dropped us right in this cool pond."

"I never used to think much of friends," Adriane slowly admitted. "I thought I didn't need them. But that's 'cause I'd never met anyone like Emily, Storm, Ozzie, or Lyra before." She gave each a shy smile.

"And Kara," Ozzie added.

"Yeah, and Kara." She looked to her friends. "Now, I couldn't imagine a day without you crazy knuckleheads in my life."

"Having friends makes everything better," Ozzie chuckled.

"Like laughing till your face hurts," Emily giggled.

"Sharing banana milk shakes," Ozzie snuggled into Emily's arm.

"Birthday parties," Zach joined in, smiling at Adriane.

"Finding a true pack mate," Lyra sat next to Zach who scratched behind her ears.

"Watching a sun rise," Emily smiled, adding to the fun.

"Making chocolate chip cookies," Ozzie licked his lips.

"Dancing to favorite songs on the radio," Lyra said, remembering mornings with Kara.

"Getting a hug." Adriane spontaneously reached over and hugged Lyra. The cat licked Adriane's cheek. Ozzie, Emily, and Zach hugged the cat at the same time, making Lyra purr with pleasure.

The laughter was contagious. It filled the halls,

wafting like light summer rain, sending pure magic into the darkness of the catacombs.

❧ ❧ ❧

The glowing strands of the fairy maps surrounded Kara, spinning in a haze of twinkling light.

"You opened the correct combination of portals at your spellsinging debut," the Dark Sorceress said in her sickeningly smooth voice. Her long, flowing robes rustled as she circled Kara, raising her arms triumphantly. "Now, show me the final portal! Show me where the source of magic lies hidden!"

Kara was terrified. What was she doing? Her mind was spinning as she watched the maps. Yet with each star that blazed to life, she felt a connection, as if she were opening another key to unlock the final treasure. She was the center of the universe in a maelstrom of magic. And it was calling to her, building in ferocity, racing through her. The wonderful power, thrilling her senses. She controlled it all! Yes, I want it!

Had she screamed aloud? She couldn't tell. Time had seemed to stop. She felt no sense of herself, only of being carried away in the flow of an oncoming tidal wave of magic. Kara felt she would be crushed under its force, sweeping her away from everything she had known, everything that was real.

Suddenly, a strange image popped into Kara's head — Ozzie with a thick creamy mustache. A banana milk shake? That ferret will eat anything! For a moment, Kara's mind was jolted free from the spellsong.

Then it was viciously yanked back.

Kara was blinded. The maps were ablaze in lights. Somewhere a wild animal shrieked. It was the sorceress. Long horns sprouted from her head, fangs protruded from her open mouth. She was screaming — but Kara could hear nothing.

Another image popped in Kara's head. This time she saw Lyra dancing on her bed, covered in her clothes. Lyra, you silly!

Something was happening. Kara could feel her fingers moving. The spell was breaking. More pictures flashed through Kara's mind — sharing a cheeseburger with Emily and hogging all the fries — Adriane handing her a bracelet, a friendship bracelet.

She heard sounds — laughing? It was Emily, and Adriane and Ozzie and . . . Lyra! They were laughing!

Kara remembered what Be*Tween had told her, *"No demon can possess you if you maintain the ability to turn and laugh at it."*

Her friends had sent her magic and she reached for it, embracing it like . . . a friend.

The spell faded. Kara quickly hid the smile that broke across her face and looked at the figure. It had turned back into the Dark Sorceress. The animal/woman was staring at her through slitted, narrowed eyes.

Can she hear them, too? Kara wondered. Quickly, Kara started waving her arms again. Without moving her head, she looked around for a way out. Then she noticed that the fairy maps had stopped spinning. They now hung in the air above her like an umbrella, winking lights flashing against the darkened ceiling.

The sorceress seemed to have noticed, too. She was eyeing the illuminated stars.

Kara followed her gaze. At the far edge of the map, one tiny light moved. It was traveling on the strands, racing nearer and nearer to Kara.

"That's it!" the sorceress said. "That is the final portal. Open it!"

Kara swung her arms wildly, keeping one eye on the approaching light. It was moving fast, getting bigger. The light was suddenly running on — legs?! No, wait. It was taking the shape of a horse. No! A *unicorn*!

The realization hit Kara hard. The Dark Sorceress had tried to use Kara to lure the unicorn to her once before. Kara remembered how the sorceress had coveted the most magical of all animals.

Now, once again, the unicorn was traveling the web, coming for her!

"No!" Kara cried. This time the cry was out of her mouth before she could stop it.

The fairy maps exploded in light. Momentarily blinded, Kara fell.

She struggled to her feet, blinking. Long hair flicked across her shoulder, but it was not the Dark Sorceress's tresses — it was a long tail.

The unicorn stood in the room, as magnificent as Kara remembered. White hide smooth as a first snowfall, rippled over its muscled body. Its long mane and tail ruffled like silk. And upon its forehead, its crystalline horn flowed with rainbow light.

The Dark Sorceress saw the unicorn at the same moment Kara did. Her eyes flew wide with rage. "What is this trickery?!"

The mighty unicorn turned its deep golden eyes at Kara. Waves of emotion surged through the girl, sure, strong, and loving.

Then, in a voice as clear as rain and powerful as the breaking dawn, it spoke. *"We must ride."*

Kara broke for the unicorn.

The sorceress was enraged. Somehow the girl had broken her binding spell! With the strength of an animal, the witch lunged at Kara.

Kara ducked. With a leap, she was on the unicorn's back, grabbing hold of his silken mane, burying her face in his neck.

The creature gave a fierce snort, reared upon its hind legs, and leaped.

In a flash of light, unicorn and rider vanished.

Chapter 13

Lyra yowled, pacing like a trapped animal. *"Kara's gone!"*

"What do you mean?" Emily asked.

"She's not in the lair anymore. I'm sure of it!"

Adriane and Emily exchanged worried glances.

"Let's not jump to conclusions," Emily said as calmly as she could.

"C'mon, we have to get out of here." Zach stood on wobbly legs.

"Okay, we'll just have to choose a direction and go." Adriane helped brace the boy.

"And end up somewhere worse?" Ozzie cried. "Who knows what's lurking in this place!"

Lyra had stopped pacing. The cat stood stock still.

"What is it, Lyra?" Emily asked.

"Something comes," Lyra said softly.

Everyone stopped.

A high-pitched howl pierced the air, echoing through the tunnel like a ghost.

Lyra turned toward the sound. Adriane grasped the cat's shoulder. Down the dark hall, the strange cry echoed. It was coming closer.

Adriane raised her wolf stone, and golden fire sparked dangerously from her wrist. "Stay behind me," she ordered.

Another howl filled the corridor, short and mournful.

Adriane crept lightly down the hall, the others close behind. She put a finger to her lips and motioned for them to stay where they were.

The howl turned into a wailing cry as Adriane slowly approached. Whatever had come was just around the corner.

With a wave of her arm, Adriane spun into position. Sweeping her stone before her, she leaped into the darkness.

There was a scuffle and a loud *yelp!*

"Adriane!" Ozzie screamed, running to their friend.

"We're rescued!" Adriane said, calmly walking back into the corridor.

Behind her, a small fuzzy head peeked around the corner.

"Dreamer!" Emily cried, elated.

The group quickly surrounded the perplexed little mistwolf, hugging and scratching, rubbing, and hugging some more. Dreamer rolled about, happily barking and wagging his tail.

"I don't know who's happier to be found, us or Dreamer," Ozzie observed.

"How'd you find us?" Adriane knelt, staring into the pup's large green eyes. The mistwolf cocked his head. Adriane's mind flashed on quick images: long, dark, scary corridors, a small wet nose sniffing the air.

"You tracked our magic?" Adriane guessed, impressed.

Dreamer barked.

"Good boy," Adriane rubbed his scruffy neck. "Can you take us to Storm?"

The pup looked over its shoulder and growled. Then he barked.

"Okay, then," Adriane looked to her friends. "Looks like Dreamer here is a natural magic tracker. Don't be scared," she said to the mistwolf. "I'm here now. Take us to Storm."

❧ ❧ ❧

Kara leaned forward atop the unicorn's broad, smooth back. The path of light beneath his alabaster hooves glowed stronger as trails of sparkling magic streamed from his mane and tail. On his forehead, his horn shone brightly, illuminated from within.

Kara saw that they were racing on the web it-self, following the pathways of magic. Beneath the unicorn's pounding hooves the endless strands shimmered with pure energy.

The unicorn did not pass *through* portals — in-stead he created them, matching the sequence of the star maps Kara had unlocked. Each portal opened a window of light in its wake, connecting the sequence along the web.

The unicorn raced faster and faster. Kara felt no fear. The unicorn drew strength from *her*, and she willed with all her heart for whatever magic she possessed to be given, freely and unconditionally. In that eternal moment, unicorn and rider became one, blazing forever across the infinite web of hope, dreams, and renewal.

One question remained.

Kara leaned forward. "Where are we going?"

Reflected from the glimmering web, glints of fire played across the unicorn's golden eyes. *"Home."*

He lowered his head and shot forward. In a blinding flash, the web disappeared.

❧　　❧　　❧

The halls were so dark they could barely see, but Adriane did not want to use her wolf stone and tip off the sorceress of their approach. Lyra ran at her side. Her feline night vision helped them keep up with the determined Dreamer. At least they were going up.

"There's something ahead," Adriane felt her jewel spark with danger. She willed the wolf stone silent.

They were approaching an open series of large caverns.

"I remember this place," Adriane whispered. "There were forges of fire where imps worked building crystals!"

But the rooms ahead were silent, spilling a soft eerie green glow into the hall. Whatever activity had gone on in there before had long been abandoned. Zach felt his way around the wall, moving across the entrance. He quickly covered his dragon stone as it flashed. Lyra sniffed the air, growling low.

They peered into the chamber, jewels splashing light across shards of broken crystals. Spots glowed an ominous green. Black fire.

Dreamer scurried back, shaking his head as if stung.

Lyra hissed, the fur on her back raised in a long ridge.

"Oh, no!" Ozzie cried.

"Don't go in there!" Adriane ordered.

The structures were all cracked and broken, their sharp edges blackened and covered in green slime. Emily shuddered. Every jagged green edge reminded her of a horrible wound. They had to be the witch's failed experiments, and the cause of the Black Fire.

"Come on, let's go," Zach urged them. "Nothing we can do here."

They continued in the tunnel making their way to the last chamber, a vast opening in the earth.

"I can feel them!" Zach cried. The stones pulsed stronger.

Adriane tried to contain her wolf stone. Surely this close the sorceress would sense the magic of the jewels. But her caution fell by the wayside as they rounded the corner, entered the immense cavern — and saw the crystals.

They could all feel them — *mistwolves trapped inside*.

Adriane quickly scanned the room for Storm. The cavern was as big as a football field, the three crystals rising in the darkness pulsed with shifting, murky greens, blacks, and grays. Something was happening since they were last here. The air was filled with electricity.

Zach touched Adriane and pointed.

On the far side of the cavern, red-eyed creatures as black as night scurried everywhere, working to keep the crystals polished. Sparks of power jumped and raced, leaping from crystal to crystal.

Emily shivered, even though it was hot in the chamber. Something tickled at the back of her mind, pushing at her, and getting more intense.

"What is it, Emily?" Ozzie asked, looking at her drawn face.

"The magic is coming," Emily answered.

Dreamer looked to Adriane. The warrior nodded, and the small mistwolf jumped onto the shallow floor.

Adriane blocked Zach with her arm. "Not that way."

"Good idea."

They circled around the opposite way, staying in the shadows at the base of the crystals.

"Storm!" Adriane cried. The silver mistwolf stood in the center of the three crystals. Her body glowed, illuminated by waves of mist that wafted into the crystals.

Adriane ran to her friend, throwing her arms around the wolf's neck — and fell to the cold, stone floor. She had fallen right through Storm as if the wolf was a ghost. Adriane scrambled to her feet, confused and worried.

"Storm?"

"My heart soars to see you, Warrior."

"Storm! What's wrong?"

"Zachariah, my son" the voice of the mistwolf Silver Eyes called.

"I'm here!" Zach's face was pressed against the crystal. "Don't speak, save your energy!"

Emily carefully walked around the crystal, examining it, touching it lightly, sending her senses into its core, as she would a sick patient.

Wolf Sister! Moonshadow's voice filled Adriane's head. *Tell your packmate to release her hold on us!*

"Storm?" Adriane looked to her friend.

"Wolf Brother," the voice of Moonshadow called out. *"You must not break the crystal!"*

"What are you talking about?" Zach asked. "We are going to get you out of there!"

"No, you cannot!" Moonshadow insisted.

"Why not?"

"We are all infected with the poison," Moonshadow said. *"We cannot be released."*

Zach gasped and turned to Adriane and Emily.

"I have held them here until your return, Healer," Storm said to Emily.

Emily flinched. There must be one hundred mistwolves in there. How could she possibly save them all? She could feel the Black Fire swirling, ripping apart the fabric of the mistwolves' magic.

"Healer," Storm said. *"You must save them."*

A sudden commotion and flashes of blue turned their attention to the sides of the cavern. Dozens of imps had left the forges, aware of the strangers' intrusion into their chamber. Sparks of electricity jumped across them. With a wail, the imps pounced like a black wave.

Lyra roared as Adriane jumped, spinning in the air, landing and rolling across their path. She pulled up into a fighting stance, wolf stone raised and blazing. With a fierce swing, she launched a ring of golden fire. The imps in front exploded in inky blobs, splattering across the floor.

Shrieking, the others ran as fast as they could to the far side of the chamber and out the door.

Emily wanted to run with them but couldn't.

"If the sorceress hasn't noticed us yet, she sure has now," Zach said.

Adriane grabbed Emily's arms. "Can you do this? Can you save them . . . and Storm?"

Emily's mouth fluttered, her heart in her throat. "I . . . I don't know."

"Emily," Ozzie was at her side. "When that magic hits, they'll be killed for sure. You have to try."

Emily looked at her friends. She was a healer, she had to act. "I need time."

"I'll get it for you," Adriane said.

"What are you going to do?" Zach asked, stumbling to her side.

"I'm going to pay a visit to the sorceress."

"I'm going with you," Zach insisted.

"No. You stay here and help Emily. She needs the power of your dragon stone."

Zach was not convinced.

"Zach," she said carefully. "You're barely healed yourself. I need room to maneuver. I can't also be worried about you."

Zach nodded. "I've seen you in action. No one's better."

A twitch of a smile played across Adriane's lips.

"I'll go with her," Lyra snarled, lips drawn in a vicious snarl. *"It's payback time!"*

No one was going to argue with that cat.

"All right." Adriane said. "Let's go!" She took a step and faltered — and turned to Storm. She could not afford the emotion. Not now. She stared at her friend. The mistwolf was transparent — fading.

"I am always with you," Storm said.

Adriane turned away and closed her eyes, letting the feelings wash through her, twisting, honing, and fine-tuning them into a laser beam of purpose and will.

Without a backward glance, she purposely strode into the corridor. If she had looked back, she would have broken, knowing that was the last time she would ever see her pack mate alive.

Chapter 14

Kara stood on the beach, watching waves rolling lazily upon the warm sands. Before her, giant flat stones etched with an intricate mosaic pattern, stretched out across the waters itself.

A silken flower grazed her cheeks with a fragrance sweeter than freesia or jasmine blooms. She turned to see dozens of floating figures. Gossamer wings seemed to catch and hold the light, reflecting it onto their flawlessly smooth faces and flowing hair — fairy wraiths. Large emerald eyes watched her.

You have come back to us, blazing star, a wraith of unimaginable beauty spoke.

"Where am I?" Kara asked. But the moment the words left her tongue, she knew. She had been here before. Was it in a dream? "Is this the final portal?" she asked in amazement.

You cannot get to Avalon through a portal, the wraith replied.

Kara felt a chill run through her body.

Only a unicorn can bring you here, another wraith fluttered close by, its long silken body almost translucent as it sparkled in the air.

A warm wind whispered past Kara's face, tickling her neck and ears. Kara looked into the large exotic eyes of the wraiths. Warmth filled her body.

Close your eyes.

Wraith voices seemed to come from everywhere at once.

Now open them.

Kara gasped as she gazed out to the mystical island, the home of all magic.

The flat bridge led to three stone rings encircling the island off shore. She could make out no details, it was completely shrouded in mist.

What do you see?

"Everything's changed," Kara breathed. "Avalon really does exist!"

It does for you.

Kara turned toward the gentle voices. "I don't understand."

You choose to see it.

Kara slowly began to understand. If you believe hard enough, dreams can come true.

"Can you release the magic and save Aldenmor?" She asked the wraiths.

Once the magic begins to flow from this place, it

cannot be stopped, a wraith said. *It could be wonderful and it could be very dangerous. Do you understand, Mage?*

"Yes," Kara said. "I mean, no." She had so many questions she wasn't sure what to ask. How was she supposed to start the magic? Would it be enough? What about the danger? And where were her friends? Were they okay? She opened her mouth, "What is a blazing star?" she finally asked.

There are a few who not only choose their own destiny but also change the path of the future forever. Those few attract magic, they guide it, strengthen it. It is up to them to guide magic along the right path. The power is not in the magic. The power is being able to choose what to do with it.

Kara nodded. She still felt unsure and suddenly shy. "I don't feel special, I just want to help my friends."

The wraiths circled her.

May you always choose wisely.

They parted, and Kara saw something shimmering in the sand. It was a scalloped, teardrop-shaped jewel — the very one Kara had found in the pond at Ravenswood so long ago. She couldn't keep it, because it was not given to her.

Kara stared at the unicorn jewel, stunned. "But I returned it to you."

You have made it yours.

She knelt and reached for the jewel, grasped it in her hand. A spark of light flashed from the stone. A magic jewel! It was everything she had ever wanted — why didn't it seem so important now? All she wanted was to find her friends, to make sure they were okay. She wanted to help save the creatures of Aldenmor and Earth.

Kara turned the jewel over in her hands. It sparkled with magic. "Thank you," she said to the wraiths. Suddenly, there were no more questions. She knew what she must do and she chose to do it.

Kara held her unicorn jewel high and concentrated. The wraiths fell away, vanishing with the wind, leaving her with a whisper — *The magic is with you, now and forever.*

Kara pictured magic, pure and good, flowing to a world that desperately needed it.

The unicorn jewel blazed with diamond-bright light. The waters around the island between the stone rings began to swirl building into waves of energy. With a rush, the whirlpool lifted into the air and streamed across the sky. Ribbons of rippling lights cascaded onto the web. It had begun.

Kara smiled — and everything vanished as she was jerked backward, pulled into the forbidden Otherworld.

The Dark Sorceress felt the wave like a jolt!

She watched the star map, hanging open like a twinkling dome. One by one, the portals flashed as magic flowed — she could feel it, coursing its way through the sequence of portals, right now heading for her crystals. She licked her lips with a pointed tongue. She would have liked once and for all to find out where the so-called "home" of magic was, but the girl had vanished before revealing the location. It didn't matter really. Magic was magic, and fairy magic happened to be quite powerful. The witch knew there were many different sources of magic. And yet, feelings of uneasiness prickled against her skin. A warning.

Another jolt!

Those fairimentals had tricked her! She had been wrong about the maps. There was no final portal. They had constructed a safety gap. The joining of the maps had called the unicorn. And that is what had found the magic.

Her blood boiled, bubbling like the tainted water in her seeing pool. The blazing star and the unicorn had been within her grasp — right here in the same room! And now they were gone.

Yet the magic *was* coming. She wasn't wrong about that. The blazing star must have released it.

Let the Skultum deal with her, she thought, robes whipping behind her as she dipped a claw into the pool. The crystals would be ready. With the mist-wolf magic slowly eaten away by the Black Fire, the flow would be drawn to their cries.

An image of a red-haired girl surfaced. Emanating from the magic stone on the girl's wrist was a strong, blue-green light. It pulsed, slowly at first and then rapidly. The light surrounded the huge crystals.

Another of those mages! How had they escaped the dungeons? For the first time in decades, the Dark Sorceress felt something worming its way through her, doubt . . . and fear.

She pounded her fist in the water, sending it flying across the floor — and over the boots of a tall dark-haired girl.

The witch stood with a start. How could this girl have gotten into her chamber past her senses? Then she noticed the large beast slinking from the shadows to stand next to the girl. The cat's eyes glowed with feral rage and its lips pulled back, revealing razor teeth.

Instantly suppressing her surprise, the sorceress carefully walked to the center of the room.

"Well, well, the warrior mage," A smile played across her thin lips. "I'll say one thing about you mages, you're stubborn."

"And you're dead meat!" Adriane's heart hammered in her chest.

"So eloquently put, but I wish you would learn some manners." The witch raised her hand, and the giant doors behind Adriane and Lyra slammed shut, locking them in the witch's chamber.

Adriane was suddenly aware of the stone wall at her back, and the fact that Stormbringer was not at her side. She didn't see any of the sorceress's serpent guards lurking about, but they could be hiding in the shadows.

The witch's eyes fixed on the wolf stone. "I know what you think you're doing, trying to by your friend some time to heal the mistwolves. But they're long gone." The sorceress's eyes sparked. "Just like your mistwolf."

Adriane faltered, stung.

"Oh, did I say something?" Her bloodred lips contorted into a wicked smile. "Your wolf is dying while we sit here and chat. And for what?"

For an instant, all Adriane wanted to do was turn and run back and fight alongside Storm. She fiercely pushed the feeling away.

"And what about you, great beast?" The sorceress swung to face Lyra. "Where's your friend, the blazing star, hmm?"

Adriane quickly scanned the room and spotted

Kara's backpack on the floor. But her friend was not there. "What have you done with her?" she demanded.

"Me? Why nothing. She has abandoned you. And as you can see," she swept her hand to the lights of the star map, "the blazing star has released magic for my crystals."

Lyra circled behind the sorceress, snarling, *You will pay for what you have done to my sisters.*

"Ah, yes," the witch extended long claws from her fingers. "I remember now. They were some of the first I tried in the crystals. I watched them carry the Black Fire for hours. And what did you do? You ran away because you couldn't help them."

Lyra roared in anger.

"Doesn't matter now. The magic comes, and it will be under my control. Do you really think you can stop me?" Her voice rose in anger. "Right now, my armies come! And with them my special warrior. You remember it, don't you?" She stared at Adriane. "It's called a manticore. Vicious creature, lethal."

Adriane signaled Lyra with her glance. The cat pounced, lunging straight for the sorceress. With a wave of the witch's hand, red fire shot across the room. Lyra's wings flew open, and she swooped into the air above the deadly magic. Purposely,

Lyra flew to the walls, as the witch followed, trying to hit the cat again. The distraction was long enough for Adriane to hide what she was doing.

"Drake!" Adriane called, raising her wolf stone in the air.

"Adriane!" the dragon's voice boomed in her head. *"There are many creatures here!"*

"Remember what I told you?"

"Yes."

"Do it. Now!"

"I help!"

"Yes, Drake, help us!" Then Adriane leaped. She spun into a circle, weaving rings of golden fire from her stone. With every ounce of strength she could muster, she forged the rings into a fireball and hurled it at the sorceress.

The witch caught the movement and blocked the oncoming magic, sending it crashing into the walls. Adriane feinted to the left, sending another fireball straight at her enemy. This one smashed into the sorceress, covering her in blazing light.

Lyra landed at Adriane's side, forcing her own strength into the warrior's jewel. Adriane spun again, building the power, throwing a third ball of magic careening into the witch. Again and again, she pounded away, screaming in rage as fire consumed the sorceress, lighting the room in a rising inferno.

Adriane spun to a stop, breathing hard, exhausted. She had not meant to unleash such excessive force. Control yourself, she told herself. Save your strength! Don't let your emotions cloud your actions!

The tower of fire that was the sorceress blazed wildly. Then it began to move, gliding across the floor. In a sudden burst, the fire lifted from the witch — revealing her untouched.

She raised a clawed finger in a spiraling motion. Adriane suddenly felt dizzy and disoriented. The room seemed to shift as the witch sent the fire slamming back against Adriane and Lyra. They were thrown against the wall and crumbled to the ground.

Pinpricks of light burst in Adriane's head. Trying to stop the room from spinning, she saw Lyra slumped on the cold floor.

"That was very good. Very good. You know why I am not going to kill you, don't you?"

Adriane watched the sorceress brush herself off as if nothing had happened.

"I'm going to build a special crystal just for you and your friends. I think your magic is quite ready for harvesting." She casually sat on her throne and laughed.

Chapter 15

Kara didn't know where she was. Walls of flowing mists surrounded her even though she walked upon solid ground. The place was eerily quiet, but she knew she wasn't alone. She could sense him before she saw him, and he — the one she had to face — was the real danger.

He had deceived her. He'd made her believe she had talent, she could sing — and instead tricked her into spellsinging. That set off the chain reaction, one portal after another opened. Now the magic was flowing — who would control it?

"Kara Davies," she finally heard the deep, velvety voice she remembered so well.

Kara turned slowly, and defiantly stared into his eyes, dark as coal, mean as a bitter winter night. He looked exactly as he had at the Ravenswood benefit concert, morphed into the body of tall, dark-haired, magnetic Johnny Conrad.

"Congratulations," he clapped his hands and bowed. "A jewel. Just what you've always wanted. Pity it won't do you any good here."

Even now, she had to remind herself, this was *not* Johnny Conrad. This creature was not even flesh and blood. This was the dark fairy — the Skultum — Be*Tween had told her about. But it didn't matter what shape he took, or what he told her. Kara's fear turned to shimmering anger. No one made a fool of Kara Davies, not even him!

There was only one way to defeat him — make him reveal his real name, trick him into saying it out loud.

Now, dressed in Johnny's signature black leather slacks and open-neck silk shirt, he took a step closer. "The blazing star, going out in a blaze of glory," he taunted. "Maybe I'll even write a song about it."

"Where are we?" Kara asked.

"This is the Otherworlds, and only one of us will leave." He spun into a dance move. "It's only fitting that we meet here. You see this is where I was trapped until freed by the — oh, you know, it's all in the family."

Kara would not flinch. There was no way she would give him the satisfaction of frightening her. "By the way," she said, forcing herself to appear calm, "You're not Johnny Conrad. So what should I call you? Your zillions of inquiring fans want to know."

"It's — HA! Uh-uh," he wagged his finger, then singsonged, "I'll never te-ell."

Kara shrugged. "Have it your way. You tricked me once, but in the end, I sent you packing."

"That's the nice thing about life, isn't it?" he sneered. "You always get a second chance."

Kara held her defiant posture. And hoped he didn't see her swallow, didn't hear her heart thudding, her mind racing.

"This will be so much fun!" He clapped his hands.

"Don't underestimate me," Kara growled. He was so cocky, so sure of himself. There had to be a way she could trick him.

He began to circle her, taunting, "You have no friends here, no winged cats, mistwolves, or fast-talking ferrets — no one to save you. Let's see you spellsing your way out of this one!"

As he babbled, Kara pressed herself, Think! Think! What would Emily do? What would Adrianne do? What would the fairies do? "Oh, I know!" she said. "Why don't we play a game?"

That got his attention. Her mind raced — could she match him, use her wits to save herself, get him to blurt his own name?

He was wily though — and expecting her to try that. She looked to her jewel and concentrated. She never had a stone of her own before. What magic did she have? What magic had she ever been able to use that —

Pop! Pop! Pop! Pop!

Colored bubbles popped in the air. That sound, which usually annoyed her, was music to her ears.

"Kee-Kee!"

The Skultum scowled as five dragonflies flew and chirped happily around his head. "What are these fairy creatures?" He demanded.

The size of small birds, they were tiny flying dragons. Red Fiona, purple Barney, blue Fred, orange Blaze, and yellow Goldie. They were fairy creatures — the kind that didn't need portals to flit from one world to another. From the start, the dragonflies had been drawn to Kara and only Kara, and she'd learned to control them. It was the only magic she'd ever really had on her own.

While the Skultum was trying to swat them away, Kara's mind was on fast-forward. The d'flies, when she asked them, could form a magic circle and create portable portals, windows the girls had used to see and talk to one another, even from different worlds.

She could make them form a circle, what else could she . . . And then it hit her. If the dragonflies could form a circle, she reasoned, could they form . . . other things, like letters?

As if they read her mind, they answered her! Kara watched, amazed, as Barney flew in a K shape; Fiona twisted into an E, Fred formed another E, Goldie formed another K, Blaze zigzagged into more Es!

Her jaw dropped!! Kara got it. She whirled around to check, but the Skultum, still trying to bat the dragonflies away, had no clue what the miraculous little creatures were doing! Did they know the Skultum's new name?

All she needed to figure out now was how to make him say it. Kara looked up, as the dragonflies buzzed over her head. She took a deep breath, and went for it. "Hey, Skultum thing," she called, "My friends love playing, like all fairy creatures."

The Skultum was intrigued. She had hit on something.

"Look!" Kara prayed this would work. She cartwheeled — the dragonflies mimicked, fluttering around her, their jeweled eyes sparkling.

She ran in a figure eight, they followed, making the same patterns in the air.

Just as Kara had hoped, the Skultum couldn't help himself. He was hopping and clapping, running around repeating their figure eights. Games were his stock in trade.

"Watch this," Kara said, "I can get them to spellspeak."

"You cannot," he said.

"Yes, I can!" she responded.

"No, you can't," he insisted.

"Betcha! Just watch."

Kara drew her fingers in the air, and formed a T. As they'd done before, two dragonflies — Fred and Blaze — formed the letter. Kara grinned, encouraging them silently.

"You try it," she urged.

His eyes lit up. "Okay." Using the forefinger of his right hand, and a half-moon shape with his left, he made the letter D. Goldie, Barney, and Fiona gleefully did the same. "This is too easy."

"Oh, wait!" Kara cried, as if she'd just thought of it. "I have the best game of all. Dragonfly charades. I think of a word, they form the letters — you have to guess!"

He threw back his head and laughed. "You slay me, Kara, you really do."

Just wait, she thought. I'm not the blazing star for nothing! She said, "I'll start."

Kara started with an easy word. The d'flies' eyes swirled with excitement as they watched her form letters.

Then with a flurry of activity, the d'flies created the letters using their little bodies.

The Skultum guessed it: "Star."

Kara graciously bowed, extending her arm.

It was his turn. He signaled the motions, they flew into formation: Barney made a circle, Fiona, the squiggly line that finished the Q. "Queen," Kara guessed what it was before they were finished.

"You go," he directed. She asked for "Flobbin."

The Skultum's next word was another easy one for Kara, "Banshee."

She still wasn't close to what she needed. She needed to make him say the name — without realizing he was doing it. A silly joke she'd made to Be*Tween came back to her when they told her what she'd have to do. Kara had quipped, "What am I supposed to stand on my head?" It was worth a shot.

"Ooookay," Kara said. "You're right. This is too easy. Let's try it . . . upside down!"

"That's preposterous —" he started, then watched her with glee. He couldn't help himself. The challenge was too, too tasty.

Kara began a cartwheel and stopped when she was balanced on her hands, upside down.

She urged the d'flies to form the letters: DOOWSNEVAR. The Skultum stood on his head and read it: RAVENSWOOD!

His upside down was: GNOSLLEPS: SPELL-SONG.

Kara was ready. She snapped her fingers and winked at the flies — they knew. "One last word — and this one's for the money."

"One for the money, two for the show — this show is over, and I get to go!" He giggled, standing on his head and watching carefully as the dragonflies formed their last word.

At the top of his lungs, he shouted, CIGAM!

His jaw dropped, his eyes bugged. Too late. He realized what he'd done.

Magic flew from the fairy, covering Kara in light. Now back in its true and horrid form, the Skultum stood frozen. Its reptilian scales glistened as it faded away.

The last words he heard were Kara's: "You won! You won!" Like a Cheshire cat, the Skultum disappeared, leaving only its surprised face. With a *Pop!* it vanished.

Kara rounded up the dragonflies. "Great work, guys."

They chattered and squeaked, twirling happily in the air.

"There's just one more thing I need," she said. The d'flies stopped in mid-twirl. *"Ooooo!"*

Chapter 16

Emily brushed her damp hair back as she stood in the center of the three crystals. The familiar feeling of hopelessness welled inside. It was mixed with a new feeling — dread. Then Emily felt something else. The room lurched and started shaking. Emily knew what it was. The wave was getting closer, rising into a crest that would crash into the crystals, washing away everything in its path.

"You did it before, Emily," Ozzie stayed behind her, close on her heels. "Remember little Vela and the elves."

Emily nodded. She had been sick, her jewel infected with the dark poison. A hundred mistwolves were infected now. This was different . . . Or was it? She could feel the pull of the Black Fire, reaching for her. But she had healed herself and in the process, she realized, had formed an immunity of sorts, a shield. Another gift from her friend, the fairy creature called Phel. Was that a dream? Had

Phel really come to her? She believed with all her heart that he had and she carried her shield like a weapon, striking at the Black Fire.

Zach stood to her left, dragon stone raised, pulsing with red power. "They're getting stronger!"

"There are too many of us!" Moonshadow called. *"Save yourselves!"*

"Keep quiet, Brother," Zach said, "You sound like a squeaky mouse."

"A mouse?! When I get out of here, I'm going to show you who's a mouse!"

"You are, that's who!" Zach goaded his wolf brother on.

Suddenly, the crystals began to pulse together in a unified rhythm.

Emily pushed harder, her stone flashing with incandescent intensity.

A second later, the massive wave of magic slammed into the room.

Emily tumbled back, overwhelmed by its power. The magic sparkled and glowed as it swirled into the crystals. Cries of agony rose from the mistwolves as magic began filling the crystals, crushing everything in its way.

There was a loud *CRACK!*

The base of one crystal had cracked! It forked and snaked its way upward. Flaming green liquid spurted from the gaps.

"Look out!" Emily screamed, dousing the poison with blazing blue light.

Flaming green droplets escaped from the glittering tower, splattering at their feet. Ozzie screamed, leaping back to avoid the burning poison.

"Healer! Run!" Moonshadow called out.

"No!" Emily shouted back.

If the enormous crystal blew apart now, the Black Fire fallout would be worse than anything the already ravaged world of Aldenmor had suffered. But if she didn't do something, the mistwolves would die.

"Zach, when I say so, split open the crystal!" Emily shouted.

"Are you sure?"

"Yes! I've stabilized most of the wolves, I'll finish the job as they come out."

"You hear that?" Zach yelled into the crystals.

"Yes," Moonshadow called back.

Without taking her eyes off the first crystal, Emily held out her arm. The rainbow jewel was blinding. "I can do this." There was not a single shred of doubt in her voice.

Ignoring the deafening rumble and the glowing green flames erupting around her, Emily pictured the mistwolves, strong and whole. She stood, firmly holding up her shield of light. "Now!"

Zach fired his dragon stone at the crystal, covering it in red. The crystal shook violently and shattered, exploding upward as if hurled from the earth itself.

Thirty mistwolves leaped into the chamber. Some fell to the ground roiling in pain. Others shook, growling and snarling.

Ignoring his wounds, Moonshadow stumbled past them, herding the wolves into the light of the healer.

"Moonshadow!" Zach recognized his pack brother at once. The wolf was badly burned, toxic green lines crisscrossed over his charred skin. Emily rushed forward, ignoring the searing poison and placed her hands directly over Moonshadow's flanks.

A shudder went through her body as she felt the great wolf's pain. Then his heartbeat locked rhythm with hers, and Emily pulled the sickness from the wolf's body. Ever so slowly, the green lines began to disappear and the flesh started to heal.

Emily whirled, covering as many wolves in healing light as fast as she could. She moved like a dancer, reaching the mistwolves with the power of her healing.

Then Zach, Emily, and Ozzie ran to the next crystal. Dragon stone raised, rainbow jewel ready, fierce fuzzy ferret face steady.

"Ready?" Zach asked.

Emily nodded. "Go!"

❧　❧　❧

Something opened and something closed in Adriane's mind at the same time. She felt mistwolves — they were free! She searched frantically through the voices in her head. But she couldn't find Storm's. She wanted to scream but was suddenly knocked to the ground as the throne room shuddered. Chunks of rock fell from the high ceiling, smashing to the polished floor.

The sorceress was on her feet moving to the seeing pool.

Adriane stood against the shaking wall. Lyra paced back and forth snarling. The cat was okay, as far as Adriane could tell.

With a stir from her finger, the Dark Sorceress conjured an image in the pool — and her eyes went wide with rage.

The wave of magic had come, but one of the crystals had exploded, leaving a cloud of magic hanging over the lair. The mistwolves had been freed!

She whirled around to the star map, watching the oncoming wave. It was unbelievable — more magic than she'd even dreamed possible.

Then she turned to Adriane. "Your friends are destroying the crystals. They would trade the lives of the mistwolves for the destruction of Aldenmor!"

"Either way, *you* won't control the magic," Adriane said cooly.

"Such a waste." The witch raised her arm, magic spinning from her long fingers. "The mistwolves cannot stand against my armies."

"Think again, loser," Adriane spat.

The sorceress's eyebrow raised in suspicion. She suddenly snapped her head as if hearing incredibly bad news and stared more closely into the pool. Her body was shimmering in rage, magic fire radiating around her.

Adriane steeled herself and faced the evil witch calmly. "What's the matter? Your monsters having a little *dragon* trouble?"

With a screech, the witch hurtled magic at Adriane. Lyra knocked the warrior to the side as it hit the wall, ricocheting around the room. Adriane flung her arms and sent golden fire back at the witch. The sorceress held up her hand, but as Adriane pushed harder, Lyra roared.

The witch's feral eyes opened wide. She was being pushed back by Adriane's power! What had happened? Adriane howled as mistwolf power surged into her jewel. But it was not enough. They were at a stalemate and they both knew the witch was more experienced.

Suddenly, bright white light spilled into the chamber — a portal opened right in the middle of the throne room! Something horrible roared. The manticore stepped through.

Adriane gasped. It was more hideous than she remembered. Hunched over, the demon creature was enormous. Its huge apelike arms rippling with muscle hung down to the floor. Legs the size of tree trunks lumbered forward as it scraped its razor-sharp claws along the stone. Fire-red demon eyes scanned the room.

The sound and the beast's foul stench made Adriane cringe.

The witch laughed. "It seems my dark creature has eluded your dragon."

Adriane slowly backed away. There was no chance of beating this thing, she was just too exhausted. She stared at the monster and — did that thing just *wink* at her?

Adriane couldn't believe it. She looked to Lyra. The cat seemed to be — *smiling?*

The witch stepped next to the manticore as the portal glowed behind her. "Take them!" she ordered.

"Oookee-dookee."

What was that?

Something fluttered. Adriane looked closer.

Fiona, the red dragonfly, was sitting on the

witch's head! The little d'fly peered into the sorceress's face. *"Peeyeww!"*

"Ahhhhhh!" the sorceress screamed, waving the creature away.

"Ahhhhh!" The little red dragonfly freaked and popped out.

Pop! Pop! Pop! Pop!

Dragonflies!

"Oooo, Dee-Dee!" Fred landed on Adriane's shoulder, nuzzling into her neck.

"What trickery is this?" the witch screamed at the manticore. "Kill them all!"

The creature's eyes flashed. It opened its razor-toothed mouth — and spoke. "I don't think so."

It wasn't the voice of a monster. It was — *Kara's* voice.

Adriane could feel the strong magic of her friend inside the thing. There was no doubt the creature was Kara.

The witch stared in shock. "How . . ."

But Adriane was already in front of her, wolf stone raised.

"Would you like to do the honors?" the monster held its twisted claws out to the portal.

Adriane stepped forward, her jewel blazing.

Shock registered across the witch's face.

Adriane looked at her jewel and lowered her arm.

"What I think she needs . . ." the warrior began, "is a little human touch."

With that, she connected — with a right cross! The witch flew backward, straight into the portal.

The dragonflies gleefully whizzed around the portal, spinning and twirling.

The manticore transformed, its huge body melting away to reveal a slim blond-haired girl in its place.

"You!" The witch stammered.

Lyra howled.

Kara waved to the sorceress. "Buh-*bye* now."

For a moment, the sorceress' eyes remained visible, radiating hatred.

The dragonflies squeaked and chirped as the portal got smaller and smaller, until with a twinkle, it vanished — taking the sorceress with it.

Kara stood wiping her hands. "Pretty smelly, huh? What?"

Adriane looked at her in shock. "That was amazing! How did you do that?"

Kara smiled and waggled a sparkling jewel in her friend's face. "I got a jewel. I got a jewel."

Adriane raised an eyebrow. But before Kara could gloat some more, Emily called out, "Adriane, come quickly!"

Chapter 17

Kara, Adriane, and Lyra entered the crystal chamber. It was in complete chaos.

Mistwolves were everywhere, howling and growling, crystal shards littered the floor, sparking and crackling. The ceiling had been blown open, the sky was visible through thick clouds of green. It hung over them, covering everything in the room with a glittering, pulsing glow.

The mistwolves all called to Adriane, who ran into the fray, looking for Zach and Storm.

"Kara!" Ozzie called. "Over here!"

Kara and Lyra found an exhausted Emily, still working to heal the wolves.

"Kara, are you all right?" Emily ran her hand over a brown-and-gray wolf and sent it on her way.

"I'm fine."

"What happened?" Emily asked.

"Never mind about me. How are you doing?" Kara wanted to know.

"The mistwolves are well enough to leave."

Emily swept back sweat-streaked hair from her face.

"What's stopping them?" Kara asked.

"They *refuse* to leave!" Zach ran to them, giving Kara a quick nod, then looked to the ceiling. "They are holding the Black Fire from spreading from this place."

The roiling fire pulsed and glowed above them. The cloud continued to darken, becoming almost black.

"I don't know what else to do!" Tears spilled down Emily's face.

"Emily!" Kara held her friend's hands, looking deep into her eyes. "Remember when I asked you how far this thing would go?"

Emily nodded, sniffling.

"And why we were chosen?"

"Yes," Emily answered.

"We *weren't* chosen." Kara said. "*We* were the ones who chose!"

Emily looked at her friend. She was right. Emily had chosen to become a healer. Adriane had chosen to follow Storm on the warrior's path. And Kara had chosen to join them.

"Now we have to follow our path wherever it leads. We each do it our own way — with the help of our friends!" Kara turned to include everyone in the room. "And we choose now to finish this!"

"She's right!" Ozzie joined in. "The magic is sick and needs to be healed, just like all of you and the other creatures of Aldenmor."

"Gather around us," Kara shouted. "Feed your magic to Emily. We will heal the magic."

Suddenly, Emily, Kara, Adriane, Ozzie, and Lyra were surrounded by a hundred mistwolves.

Emily rolled up her sleeves and concentrated. The rainbow jewel began to pulse with blue-green light. But the light was duller than usual, dimmed by the ominous black cloud overhead.

"Concentrate on building the light," Emily told them.

Silence filled the room. The mistwolves used their magic, sending it into Emily's stone.

Ozzie's whiskers twitched as he hugged Emily tight. The rainbow jewel brightened, then pulsed.

Lightning flashed across the clouds, sending wild magic flying. The chamber walls shuddered as one collapsed, sending dust and debris everywhere.

"Stay together," Moonshadow ordered.

Kara turned to Adriane. "Are you ready?"

Adriane stood next to Kara and held out her hand.

Kara grasped it. "Ready, Emily?"

Emily nodded, placing her hand over those of her friends.

Emily raised her rainbow jewel, sending blue fire up and around her arms. Adriane raised her wolf stone, golden fire wrapping around her and twisting over Emily's blue magic into a tight bond.

Then Kara held up her stone. It blazed like a diamond.

Everyone watched in amazement as blue and gold fire raced around Kara, covering her in magic.

"Let's do it!" she yelled, and let the magic go.

Silver fire burst from the unicorn jewel streaming like a rocket into the clouds above.

The cloud formed into a whirlpool of power.

With all of their hearts, the three mages focused their will.

Suddenly, the clouds exploded upward and streaming rays of multicolored lights lit the sky.

The chamber rocked as another wall collapsed.

"Let's get out of here!" Ozzie yelled.

The mistwolves bolted, running from the chamber in a wave. Emily grabbed Ozzie, hoisting him into her arms as Kara and Lyra herded the final wolves out.

Dust flew and the rumbling grew louder.

"Adriane!" Kara screamed, grabbing the warrior and pushing her from the chamber.

"Storm!" Adriane called out, but heard no reply, only silence echoing from the emptiness in her heart.

"We have to go now!" Kara pulled Adriane from the chamber and into the hall.

With a thunderous boom, the chamber behind them collapsed in a pile of rubble.

The girls burst through the front doors and into the bright light of the Shadowlands.

The mistwolves fanned out to make sure no guards or monsters stood in their way. Nothing did. Word had spread fast. The reign of the Dark Sorceress was over.

"Zach!" Drake swooped down from the sky, stirring up a dust storm as he landed. Zach ran to his friend, hugging the dragon tight.

The group made its way to the top of the dunes and looked to the skies.

It was incredible! Bands of light drifted overhead, brightening to form giant curtains rippling with reds, blues, oranges, and purples. The entire sky seemed full of color and motion. Bright points of light swirled like pinwheels as magic rained from the sky.

The magic drifted through the air, over the Shadowlands, bathing everything in a fine, shimmering mist. The healing of Aldenmor had begun.

As the group watched, the land began to transform. Dry, blackened earth drank in the magic and sprouted tender grasses and wildflowers. Charred tree and shrub branches burst with lush leaves.

Emily felt giddy, hugging Ozzie tightly, laughing and crying at the same time. She let the rain wash over her, never wanting this feeling to end.

Kara sat next to Lyra, hugging her friend close. She took a deep breath, inhaling fragrant spring blossoms. In her hands, the unicorn jewel felt warm.

Zach stood next to Drake, the big dragon refusing to let the boy leave his side.

The mistwolves surrounded them, howling in song, reveling in the healing of their planet. But then the wolfsong grew somber, filled with sadness and loss.

To the side of the dune, Adriane stood alone watching the magical light show.

Kara, Emily, Lyra, and Ozzie went to Adriane's side.

Tears welled in Emily's blue eyes. "There was nothing you could have done," she said, as if reading her friend's mind.

"I know," Adriane said.

"Storm saved us all," Moonshadow said, slowing approaching Adriane, Zach at his side.

Kara and Emily put their arms around Adriane as the warrior leaned into them.

"No tears." Adriane wiped at her eyes. "She wouldn't want that."

"One mistwolf held a hundred of us," Moonshadow said. *"Do you know how she did that?"*

Adriane looked at the large black wolf.

"She held us until we were safe because she was thinking of you. Her love for you gave her the strength."

"Thank you," Adriane smiled.

"We weep for your loss, Warrior."

The group was startled at the new voice they heard.

"You have guided magic back to the fairy glen." The voices of the fairimentals echoed in their heads. *"And you have changed the future forever."*

Epilogue

W*arrior."*

Adriane stood in the meadow under the shade of the great tree, Okawa. Its branches glistened with greens as if it, too, rejoiced in the coming rains. But the bright rippling colors were in stark contrast to the rain that fell in Adriane's heart. Around her a hundred mistwolves, the entire pack, had gathered.

Moonshadow, Silver Eyes, and Zach approached her.

"Will you lead us in the wolf song?" Moonshadow asked. *"We will wish Stormbringer well on her journey to the spirit pack."*

Adriane was honored to lead the sacred ritual, reserved for members of the pack only. She threw her head back and sang the wolf song from deep in her soul as it had been taught to her by her lost friend. The pack joined, sending their voices echoing across the Fairy Glen.

Slowly, the mistwolves walked away. Adriane, Zach, Moonshadow, and Silver Eyes stood watching soft grasses and rainbow flowers wave under the light breeze.

"I can't say good-bye," Adriane whispered.

"You don't have to," Zach said gently.

"She is not lost to us, but a part of the spirit pack," Moonshadow said.

"If you listen, they speak to us still from within." Silver Eyes brushed Adriane's side.

Adriane ran her hand over her wolf mother's soft fur.

"Hold on tight to every memory, Little Wolf Daughter," Silver Eyes said. *"It is what makes your heart strong."*

Adriane closed her eyes and let the memories come — memories of her and Storm. The first time she realized they could communicate. The two of them wrestling across the hills of Ravenswood. Storm helping her understand the magic, and friendship. And their journey — together and separately — to Aldenmor.

"When does it stop hurting?" Adriane struggled to stay strong.

"Not for a long time," Zach said. "But you go on and you *hold* on! Think about what Storm would want for you."

"I don't know if I can," Adriane said truthfully. Her heart lay in pieces, locked away in a place she could not reach.

"Little Wolf," Silver Eyes said. *"You must not close your heart to those who love you."*

From the corner of her eye Adriane caught movement. Silver Eyes was nuzzling a fuzzy mistwolf pup forward. *"It is time for the student to become the teacher,"* the wolf mother said.

Dreamer was in front of her, shifting shyly on his white paws. The wolf pup lifted his head to the warrior mage.

Adriane knelt and looked into the pup's deep green eyes. "I guess we're both alone now," she whispered.

Dreamer understood. He moved into Adriane's arms. Feelings flashed — anger, fear, sadness, and loss — but underneath, tenderness and beauty, the promise of hope, and a conviction to fight for love, the heart of a warrior.

Holding Dreamer in her arms, Adriane cried. Her tears fell with the rain from her heart.

"I'll always be with you."

Dreamer's wolf eyes filled with love. And the bond was forged like iron between the lone wolf and the lone warrior — forever.

The Fairy Glen was packed.

Pegasi, wommels, brimbees, jeeran, all the magical animals from Ravenswood had returned to a place they thought they'd never see again. The waters of the fairy lake sparkled and glistened, reflecting the bright colors of the sky and the shimmering white of the portal that hung open near the shore. The wondrous Fairy Glen, seen by so few, was renewed. The heart of Aldenmor beat strong once again.

Ozzie stood chattering with a group of wide-eyed elves, astonished to be at such an extraordinary place. Emily, Kara, and Lyra waited patiently as Adriane approached with Zach, Moonshadow, and Silver Eyes. Emily smiled as she noticed Dreamer walking protectively at the dark-haired girl's side.

No words were spoken. Just a warm embrace by each told Adriane how much she was loved, how much she was needed.

"The prophecy has come to pass." The wistful windy voice belonged to Ambia, an air fairimental. A thicket of twigs, brush, and leaves then tumbled together as Gwigg, an earth fairimental, appeared.

The entire glade hushed at the presence of such magical creatures.

"Three mages have come to our aid and healed

Aldenmor," Ambia said. "*One has followed her heart, and found strength.*" The fairimental flitted over Adriane.

"*One has seen in darkness and found light,*" Gwigg rolled by Emily.

"*And one has changed completely and found —*"

"A jewel!" Kara mouthed to her friends, holding up her unicorn jewel now secured to her silver necklace.

"*— restraint!*" Ambia twinkled.

"Oh, that, too." Kara said, smiling.

"*You changed from the prettiest to the ugliest,*" Lyra teased.

"Yeah, but I'm back. And I'm still a princess!" Kara giggled.

"*The rain falls, covering Aldenmor with glorious magic,*" Ambia continued. "*It is full of possibilities and also fraught with dangers.*"

"*The Dark Sorceress has been exiled to the Otherworlds,*" Gwigg rumbled. "*But even now, magic trackers and unspeakable creatures of evil are gathering to seek out and control the magic.*"

"*So it begins, mages,*" Ambia whispered.

The voices of the fairimentals echoed in the girls' heads. *You have the power. . . . Guide the magic along the right path.*

The portal shimmered as blue-green oceans appeared. Gusts of water erupted as sea dragons, with merfolk upon their backs, burst free and arched into the air.

"We stand with you, Mags!" Kee-Lyn called from the back of Meerka.

"As do we!" The picture changed to show hundreds of elves standing atop rolling green hills and raising their arms in cheers.

"*Ozymandius,*" Ambia called out.

Ozzie shuffled forward and kneeled before the wisp of wind.

"*For your heroism and loyalty, you are hereby decreed a Knight of the Circle. Rise, Sir Ozymandius.*"

A twinkle of light suddenly glowed in the ferret's hands. When the light faded, Ozzie held a glittering golden stone. His eyes widened. "A ferret stone!" he shouted, showing his jewel to the astonished elves nearby.

Everyone cheered at this amazing honor. Crusp and Tonin and the rest of Ozzie's relatives proudly puffed up their chests, patting their newly famous elf kin on the back.

"Thanks! But . . . can I change back to my real body?" Ozzie scratched his ear.

Ambia circled the ferret like a glittering breeze. "*If you choose to stay here on Aldenmor, you may return to your elf body and honor us with your service.*"

"Yes!"

"But if you chose to return with the mages, you must remain as you are."

"Oh." Ozzie looked to the elves and turned to Emily.

Emily bit her lip.

Ozzie shuffled back and forth, fraught with indecision. "What should I do?" he asked, clearly torn.

"What you've always told us, Ozzie," Emily smiled. "You have to follow your heart."

Ozzie's brow crinkled as he clutched his new jewel and walked to the elf clan.

The animals of Ravenswood were crowded around Kara, admiring her unicorn jewel.

"It is magnificent," Balthazar said.

"Yeah, it sure is!" Then Kara smiled humbly. "Thank you, but you guys are the ones who deserve this, not me."

"Nonsense," Rasha said. "Your magic shines from within, the jewel is just a reflection of your beauty."

"Thank you." Kara hugged the animals that had become so close to her over the past months.

"Kara." Gwigg tumbled to a halt near her feet. *"The blazing star faces the hardest lessons of all in the days ahead."*

"Right, but what about the Skultum's magic?"

Kara queried. "You know, that fairy stuff about absorbing its powers."

"It is hard to say if you will keep it. You are not skilled enough to sustain that level of power," Gwigg responded.

"I see," Kara scrunched her nose. The jewel warmed and flashed — and her hair turned bright purple!!

"Ooo!" the animals admired her choice of color.

Quickly, before anyone else could notice, she turned her hair back to blonde.

"The magic runs deep inside you now," Gwigg warned. *"It is a gift. To use your powers impulsively only makes you more and more dependent on them. You must stand strong lest you fall under its darker pull."*

"What do I do?" Kara asked, suddenly worried.

"Stand strong with your friends," Ambia advised, leading Kara to the bright light.

Kara walked to the portal next to Adriane and Emily. The three girls clasped hands.

Ozzie and the elves were in deep conversation, then did a lot of hugging and more hugging. Emily watched as the ferret moved away from the elves to stand next to her.

"I'm going to miss you, Ozzie," Emily sniffled.

"Why, where are you going?" Ozzie looked confused, then smiled. "'Cause wherever it is, I'm going, too."

Kara, Lyra, Emily, Ozzie, Adriane, and Dreamer stood before the portal that would take them home. As the rainbow of lights twinkled in the skies over the Fairy Glen, they knew one thing for sure. Their friendship would see them through any new challenges and adventures they would face in the struggles ahead. The magic of Avalon had been released. But the mages had learned that the power to triumph over evil was ultimately not in the magic itself, but something more powerful: the magic of the ties that bound humans and animals, nature, and all living things — that is the spirit of Avalon.